Santa Raptor's Jolly Carnage

Santa Raptor's Jolly Carnage

Matthew Petchinsky

Santa Raptor's Jolly Carnage: A Dino-Claus Christmas Tale

By: Matthew Petchinsky

Introduction: The Legend of Santa Raptor

In the frosty silence of a long-forgotten age, deep within the cretaceous forests where the first snowflakes danced among towering ferns, a legend was born. This was no ordinary tale of prehistoric survival or the triumph of apex predators—it was the birth of Santa Raptor, a figure of mystery, magic, and merry mayhem.

It is said that millions of years ago, a peculiar velociraptor was unlike any other in its time. While most of its kind were fiercely territorial and ruthlessly efficient hunters, this particular velociraptor, known as Raptorus Claus in whispered myths, exhibited a curious nature. Instead of preying solely for sustenance, Raptorus showed an inexplicable fascination with sharing—yes, sharing! He would stash away gleaming treasures like iridescent shells, vibrant feathers, and glittering stones not for himself but to distribute to his pack and the smaller creatures of the forest. In a world ruled by tooth and claw, Raptorus's actions seemed almost...kind.

But nature is rarely kind to the kindhearted. One fateful winter, an unexpected meteor shower turned the sky into a blazing inferno, wiping out the dominant dinosaurs and plunging the Earth into an ice-covered slumber. It was in this moment of cataclysmic change that the magic of the universe intervened. The spirit of Raptorus Claus, infused with his unique blend of ferocity and generosity, did not perish with his body. Instead, it transformed, preserved by the cosmic forces at play, and became something immortal—something mythical.

Eons passed. Humanity emerged, carving out their own myths and traditions in the icy tundras and verdant valleys of their new world. One of these traditions was Christmas, a celebration of giving, joy, and the triumph of light over the darkest nights of winter. Little did the early humans know, their folklore was unknowingly influenced by a force older than time itself.

Santa Raptor's transition into the Christmas mythos is shrouded in mystery, but the pieces of the puzzle reveal themselves in fragments. Ancient cave paintings, some dating back over 10,000 years, depict a curious figure: a raptor-like creature pulling a sleigh carved from bone, its claws clutching what appear to be gifts wrapped in hides. These prehistoric depictions show the creature delivering these gifts to families huddled in their caves, yet ominously, they also show smaller figures—naughty ones—being dragged into the shadows, never to return.

Legends of Santa Raptor evolved alongside human culture. In the dark ages, he was whispered of as a fearsome guardian of justice, rewarding the virtuous and punishing the wicked. Parents would warn misbehaving children, "If you don't behave, Santa Raptor will come for you." Over time, this terrifying figure softened in the stories told to children, his fearsome image replaced with a more benevolent one in modern retellings. Yet, those who dig deeper into ancient folklore know the truth: Santa Raptor is no gentle giver, but a primal force of balance, ensuring that good deeds are rewarded and maliciousness is eradicated—quite literally.

His sleigh, crafted from the bones of the mighty dinosaurs he once ruled alongside, is said to be pulled by ghostly pterodactyls whose wings shimmer with the magic of the Aurora Borealis. His claws, sharp enough to cut through the thickest snowdrifts, leave trails of deep gouges in the earth, a mark of his passage. And his eyes—gleaming orbs of crimson light—pierce the darkness as he hunts for those who dare to cross into the realm of naughtiness.

Yet Santa Raptor is not without his charm. To the nice boys and girls, he brings gifts that are said to carry the magic of ancient times: toy dinosaurs that roar when the moon is full, shimmering crystals imbued with prehistoric energy, and hand-carved treasures that no modern craftsman could replicate. These gifts are not just tokens of goodwill; they are imbued with the very spirit of Raptorus Claus, a reminder that kindness, even in the harshest of worlds, is a gift worth cherishing.

So, as the snow falls and the wind whispers through the trees, know that Santa Raptor is watching. He doesn't need cameras or spies; his instincts, honed over millions of years, can sense the faintest tremor of mischief or the smallest act of generosity. He is more than a legend; he is a force, as old as the Earth itself, blending the primal energy of the dinosaurs with the warmth and wonder of Christmas.

This Christmas, remember: kindness is rewarded, and naughtiness is not without consequence. For when the stars align and the sleigh of bones glides across the winter sky, you may hear the haunting jingle of prehistoric bells and the low, guttural growl of the most unusual Santa to ever roam the Earth—Santa Raptor.

Chapter 1: The Sleigh of Bones

In the heart of a forgotten tundra where ancient winds carve melodies into the ice, there lies a cavern cloaked in eternal frost. This cavern, known only to the most daring adventurers as the Bone Hollows, serves as Santa Raptor's secret workshop. It is here that the legendary Sleigh of Bones was crafted, a testament to the primal creativity and ancient power of Santa Raptor.

The Vision of the Sleigh

The Sleigh of Bones is no ordinary sleigh. It is a marvel of prehistoric engineering and mystical energy, a vessel designed to withstand both the physical and metaphysical demands of Santa Raptor's eternal mission. Legend has it that the sleigh's design came to Raptorus Claus in a dream during the cataclysm that ended the age of dinosaurs. The vision was vivid: a sleigh constructed from the remains of his fallen kin, powered by the elemental forces of the Earth itself, and capable of traveling across dimensions, weaving between the present and the primordial past.

Gathering the Materials

Crafting the Sleigh of Bones was no simple feat. Santa Raptor scoured the ancient lands, guided by an unexplainable pull toward the most sacred and powerful fossils. The sleigh's framework is said to be made from the ribs of a Titanosaurus, its size and strength symbolizing the endurance required for his cosmic journey. The runners are carved from the femurs of a Triceratops, polished to a smooth, glistening finish by millennia of glacial erosion.

To bind the bones together, Santa Raptor used sinews from the remains of a woolly mammoth, preserved in permafrost. These sinews, imbued with prehistoric resilience, ensure the sleigh's flexibility and durability against the harshest conditions, from the icy winds of the Arctic to the scorching heat of volcanic regions.

The Heart of the Sleigh: The Prehistoric Gemstone

At the center of the sleigh lies its most magical component: a glowing gemstone, unearthed from the impact site of the meteor that ended the age of dinosaurs. This gemstone, pulsating with the raw energy of the cosmos, serves as the sleigh's power source. Known as the "Cretaceous Heart," it channels the energies of the Earth's ley lines, allowing Santa Raptor to soar through the skies with unparalleled speed and agility. The gemstone also grants the sleigh its ability to phase between dimensions, enabling Santa Raptor to slip into and out of homes undetected.

The Construction Ritual

The construction of the sleigh was not merely a physical endeavor but also a deeply spiritual one. Santa Raptor performed a ritual beneath the light of a rare celestial alignment, when the planets aligned to form the shape of a raptor's claw. This ritual, blending ancient instincts with newfound magical prowess, bound the sleigh's components together with an unbreakable bond.

During the ritual, Santa Raptor roared into the frozen night, a sound so powerful it cracked glaciers and echoed through time itself. This roar, infused with his intent and primal energy, awakened the sleigh, imbuing it with a consciousness of its own. Though silent, the Sleigh of Bones seems to respond to Santa Raptor's will, gliding effortlessly through the air and adjusting its course with uncanny precision.

The Prehistoric Pterodactyl Team

Of course, even the most magical sleigh needs a team to pull it. Instead of reindeer, Santa Raptor employs a flock of spectral pterodactyls, their ethereal forms shimmering like the northern lights. These prehistoric flyers, tethered to the sleigh with enchanted sinew reins, are bound by an ancient pact to assist Santa Raptor on his journeys. Their wings, translucent and glowing with an inner light, beat soundlessly, carrying the sleigh with a speed that defies comprehension.

Each pterodactyl has a name whispered in ancient tongues, their identities as much a part of the legend as Santa Raptor himself. Names like "Skyrend," "Frostwing," and "Shadowglide" evoke their ghostly presence, a reminder of the age they hail from. Their connection to the sleigh is both magical and symbiotic, as the energy of the Cretaceous Heart sustains their ghostly forms.

The Magic in Motion

When the sleigh takes to the skies, it is a sight to behold. The bones seem to glow faintly, resonating with the energy of the Cretaceous Heart. As the spectral pterodactyls pull it through the night, a trail of shimmering light—part aurora, part stardust—follows in its wake, painting the sky with prehistoric wonder. The sleigh is silent to those who are good at heart, its passage marked only by the faint jingle of enchanted bells crafted from ankylosaurus tail clubs. For the naughty, however, the approach of the Sleigh of Bones is heralded by a chilling growl that freezes the very soul.

A Balance of Power

The Sleigh of Bones is more than just a tool; it is a symbol of balance between light and darkness, generosity and justice. Its bones remind Santa Raptor of the fragility of life and the importance of kindness, while its speed and ferocity serve as a warning to those who stray into naughtiness.

As it glides through the frosty skies on Christmas Eve, the Sleigh of Bones carries with it the spirit of an age long past and the hope of a world that values goodness. It is not merely a sleigh—it is an enduring reminder that even the most fearsome creatures can embrace the magic of giving.

Chapter 2: Dino Elves and the Workshop

Deep within the icy caverns of Bone Hollows lies a place of vibrant, bustling activity—a prehistoric wonderland that defies time and logic. This is Santa Raptor's workshop, a space teeming with life, energy, and the tireless efforts of his tiny but industrious helpers: the Dino Elves.

The Birth of the Dino Elves

The Dino Elves, unlike the spectral pterodactyls that pull Santa Raptor's sleigh, are very much alive and tangible. They are a curious blend of magic and evolution, creatures born from the fossilized remains of small dinosaurs infused with the cosmic energy of the Cretaceous Heart. Standing no taller than a human toddler, these miniature dinos possess sharp claws, colorful scales, and eyes that sparkle with intelligence and mischief.

Each Dino Elf is unique, reflecting the species from which it originated. There are tiny triceratops-like elves with stubby horns, raptor-like elves with nimble hands for crafting, and even miniature stegosaur elves who use their plated tails to carry tools and materials. They are not mere servants but a lively community bound by loyalty to Santa Raptor and an unquenchable enthusiasm for their work.

The Workshop: A Prehistoric Wonderland

Santa Raptor's workshop is a marvel of both natural wonder and ancient ingenuity. Located in the heart of the Bone Hollows, the workshop is built into a vast network of interconnected caverns. The walls glisten with crystalline frost, and glowing veins of iridescent minerals provide a soft, magical light. Fossilized remains of long-extinct creatures are embedded in the walls, their presence a reminder of the prehistoric past that shaped this unique operation.

The workshop is divided into several bustling zones, each tailored to a specific aspect of Santa Raptor's mission:

1. **The Giftsmith Cavern**: This is the heart of the operation, where Dino Elves work tirelessly to create gifts for the nice boys and girls. Using tools made from volcanic rock and meteorite fragments, they craft toys, ornaments, and treasures imbued with prehistoric magic. Tiny raptor elves are especially skilled at intricate tasks, such as carving delicate patterns or assembling moving parts.

2. **The List Chamber**: Here, the Dino Elves manage the Naughty and Nice lists. The lists are written on scrolls made from ancient papyrus plants preserved in permafrost. A special group of elves known as the "List Keepers" monitor the behavior of children worldwide through enchanted amber orbs that display real-time images. These orbs hum softly, glowing green when a child performs a good deed and red when they misbehave.

3. **The Fossil Forge**: This cavern is dedicated to the creation of magical artifacts and components for the Sleigh of Bones. The forge is fueled by a never-extinguishing flame, believed to have originated from the meteor that brought the Cretaceous Heart to Earth. Dino Elves with thick, armor-like scales work here, using their strength to shape ancient materials into tools and magical devices.

4. **The Feeding Hollow**: Even Dino Elves need to eat, and this space serves as their communal dining area. They feast on berries, nuts, and roots that they cultivate in underground gardens illuminated by bioluminescent fungi. Occasionally, they roast prehistoric fish on open fires, their laughter echoing through the caverns.

The Mischievous Nature of Dino Elves

Though endlessly hardworking, the Dino Elves are also known for their playful, sometimes mischievous personalities. They delight in practical jokes, such as hiding tools from one another or swapping labels on the Naughty and Nice lists to create harmless confusion. Their antics never interfere with their duties, as they have a deep respect for Santa Raptor and his mission.

One notable prank involved painting the spectral pterodactyls in bright holiday colors just before Santa Raptor's annual flight. While the Sleigh of Bones looked more festive than ever, the prank earned the elves a stern growl from their prehistoric leader. Despite this, Santa Raptor's twinkling eyes betrayed his amusement, and the Dino Elves were forgiven after promising to repaint the pterodactyls back to their ghostly hues.

The Dino Elves' Loyalty to Santa Raptor

The bond between Santa Raptor and the Dino Elves is unbreakable. They see him not as a boss but as a guardian and a leader who has given them purpose. In return, they devote themselves entirely to ensuring his mission succeeds. The elves' loyalty extends to their vigilance in maintaining the balance of justice. They take their role as stewards of the Naughty and Nice lists seriously, often debating among themselves whether certain behaviors warrant inclusion on either list.

For instance, if a child pulls a harmless prank, the Dino Elves may argue about whether the act stems from genuine mischief or playful creativity. Their discussions are often animated, but they always come to a fair decision, guided by their innate sense of justice and a deep understanding of Santa Raptor's principles.

The Magic of Collaboration

What makes the Dino Elves truly remarkable is their ability to work together seamlessly despite their differences. Each elf brings unique skills to the table, and their collaboration results in creations that are both magical and meaningful. From toys that roar like real dinosaurs to enchanted crystals that glow softly in the dark, the gifts they produce are infused with the spirit of giving and the magic of their ancient origins.

A Community Unlike Any Other

The workshop is more than just a workplace; it is a home for the Dino Elves, a sanctuary where they can thrive and express their individuality. During their downtime, the elves sing prehistoric carols, dance around fossilized trees decorated with glowing amber ornaments, and share stories of their adventures in the Bone Hollows.

For the Dino Elves, their greatest joy comes from the knowledge that their efforts bring happiness to children around the world. They take immense pride in their work, knowing that each toy, trinket, and treasure they create carries with it a piece of their prehistoric magic and a reminder of the enduring spirit of Christmas.

As the holiday season approaches, the workshop hums with activity. The Dino Elves scurry about, their claws clicking against the icy floors as they prepare for Santa Raptor's grand flight. With their combined efforts, the magic of the Bone Hollows comes alive, ready to spread joy—or enforce justice—across the world.

Chapter 3: The Nice and the Naughty

In the intricate world of Santa Raptor, the line between "nice" and "naughty" is drawn with precision, guided by principles as old as time. Unlike the human Santa Claus, whose lists may be influenced by cultural norms or subjective judgments, Santa Raptor's criteria are rooted in primal instincts of fairness, justice, and survival—a system as unyielding as the bones that form his sleigh.

The Criteria for the Lists

Santa Raptor's judgment is not arbitrary. Over countless millennia, his Dino Elves have refined the Naughty and Nice lists into a meticulous system of evaluation. Each child's actions are assessed not only for their immediate impact but also for their underlying intent. This ensures that genuine goodness is rewarded and deliberate malice is met with appropriate consequences.

The Nice List: Traits and Behaviors

- **Kindness**: Acts of selflessness, such as helping a friend in need or showing compassion to animals, are highly valued. Santa Raptor particularly admires children who go out of their way to make the world a better place, even in small ways.
- **Courage**: Standing up for others, especially in the face of adversity, earns a place on the Nice list. This reflects Santa Raptor's respect for bravery, a trait essential for survival in the prehistoric world.
- **Honesty**: Truthfulness and integrity are cornerstones of Santa Raptor's criteria. Children who admit their mistakes and strive to make amends are seen as genuinely nice.

- **Respect for Nature**: As a being deeply connected to the Earth, Santa Raptor values children who show care for the environment, whether by planting trees, cleaning up litter, or treating animals with kindness.

The Naughty List: Traits and Behaviors

- **Cruelty**: Acts of deliberate harm, whether to other children, animals, or the environment, are swift tickets to the Naughty list. Santa Raptor has no tolerance for bullying or destructive behavior.
- **Deceit**: Persistent lying or manipulation for personal gain lands children squarely in the naughty category. To Santa Raptor, deception represents a betrayal of trust, a grave offense in the prehistoric code of ethics.
- **Greed**: Selfishness and hoarding without consideration for others are frowned upon. Sharing and cooperation were essential for survival in Santa Raptor's era, and he expects the same values in modern times.
- **Disrespect**: Rudeness, disobedience, and lack of gratitude, especially toward caregivers, signal a lack of the core values Santa Raptor holds dear.

The Role of the Dino Elves

The Dino Elves play a crucial role in maintaining the Naughty and Nice lists. Using their enchanted amber orbs, they observe children throughout the year, documenting actions and categorizing them with painstaking detail. The amber orbs allow the elves to see not just what children do, but why they do it, revealing intent and emotions behind every deed.

The elves also hold debates about borderline cases. For example, if a child takes a cookie from the jar without asking but shares it with a younger sibling, the elves might weigh the act of sharing against the rule-breaking. These discussions ensure that the lists are fair and nuanced, leaving no room for doubt when Santa Raptor takes flight on Christmas Eve.

The Consequences of the Lists

The impact of being on either list is profound. Santa Raptor's mission is to maintain balance, and his methods reflect this dual purpose.

Rewards for the Nice List For the children who embody the traits of kindness, courage, honesty, and respect, Santa Raptor brings magical gifts unlike any other. These gifts are not just toys but treasures imbued with prehistoric energy. A few examples include:

- **Amber Crystals**: Small, glowing stones that emit warmth and light, bringing comfort during the darkest nights.
- **Dinosaur Figurines**: Intricately crafted toys that roar or move when held, serving as symbols of bravery and imagination.
- **Enchanted Keepsakes**: Items that resonate with the child's personality, such as a necklace that glows when the wearer performs an act of kindness or a pouch that fills with seeds for planting when scattered on the ground.

These gifts inspire children to continue their good deeds and remind them of the joy that comes from being kind and thoughtful.

Punishments for the Naughty List For those on the Naughty list, the consequences are far more severe. Santa Raptor is not one to leave a warning note or a lump of coal. His prehistoric justice is swift and decisive:

- **The Growl of Warning**: Before taking action, Santa Raptor emits a low, guttural growl outside the homes of naughty children. This sound, deep and resonant, shakes the very ground and fills the air with an ancient, primal dread. It serves as a final warning—a chance to reform before it's too late.

- **The Shadow of the Claw**: If the warning is ignored, Santa Raptor's shadow appears, a fleeting glimpse of his fearsome form. Naughty children often feel his presence long before they see him, an ominous reminder of the consequences of their behavior.
- **Disappearance of the Naughty**: In the most extreme cases, Santa Raptor enforces his justice by removing the naughtiest children entirely. The legend holds that these children are taken to the Bone Hollows, where they must work alongside the Dino Elves as penance, learning the values of hard work, kindness, and cooperation. While these children are never harmed, their time in the workshop serves as a transformative experience, instilling in them the lessons they failed to learn on their own.

Redemption and Hope

One of the most remarkable aspects of Santa Raptor's system is its focus on redemption. Naughty children are not doomed forever. Those who learn from their mistakes and show genuine change can find themselves on the Nice list the following year. Santa Raptor, despite his ferocity, believes in second chances, a trait that reflects his deep understanding of the complexities of human nature.

Parents often use stories of Santa Raptor's justice to encourage good behavior, knowing that his legend holds a mix of awe and terror. Children, in turn, strive to stay on the Nice list, motivated by the promise of magical gifts and the avoidance of a visit from the prehistoric enforcer of Christmas traditions.

A System of Balance

The Nice and Naughty lists are more than just tools for rewarding or punishing behavior; they are a reflection of Santa Raptor's mission to maintain balance in the world. His dual role as a giver of joy and a bringer of justice ensures that goodness prevails while discouraging malice.

As the holiday season approaches, the Dino Elves work tirelessly to finalize the lists, knowing that Santa Raptor's decisions will shape the lives of children around the world. In the end, the legend of Santa Raptor reminds us all that kindness and fairness are timeless values, as enduring as the bones that form his sleigh and the spirit that fuels his mission.

Chapter 4: Christmas Eve Hunting Grounds

On the most magical—and terrifying—night of the year, Santa Raptor leaves the icy sanctuary of the Bone Hollows to embark on his dual mission of delivering joy to the virtuous and justice to the wicked. Unlike the traditional Santa Claus, who glides across the world indiscriminately, Santa Raptor's route is far more calculated. Guided by ancient instincts and the meticulous work of his Dino Elves, he identifies his "hunting grounds" for Christmas Eve: the places where he will reward the nice and punish the naughty.

Mapping the World

Santa Raptor's journey begins long before Christmas Eve. For months, the Dino Elves track and update the Naughty and Nice lists, pairing each name with a precise location. These lists are then transferred to the **Map of Justice**, an enormous, enchanted map carved into the icy floor of the List Chamber. The map's surface shifts and glows, dynamically updating as new behavior is observed.

The **Map of Justice** is no ordinary map. It incorporates not just geographical information but also layers of emotional and moral energy. Nice regions glow with a warm, golden light, while naughty areas pulse ominously in shades of red. The intensity of the glow reflects the concentration of nice or naughty children, helping Santa Raptor prioritize his stops.

Santa Raptor doesn't work alone in this endeavor. His connection to the Dino Elves and their amber orbs allows him to access real-time information about behavior changes, ensuring his route is as accurate as possible when Christmas Eve arrives.

The Selection of Hunting Grounds

Santa Raptor divides his stops into three distinct types, based on the behavior trends of each area:

1. **Golden Zones**

   These are neighborhoods or regions where the majority of children are on the Nice list. In these areas, Santa Raptor's visit is a joyous event. He swoops down silently in his Sleigh of Bones, leaving gifts in homes where kindness, courage, and honesty have prevailed throughout the year. Golden Zones are often marked by harmonious communities, where children and families work together to create a positive environment.

   Example: The Little Village of Glowridge

Glowridge, nestled in a snowy valley, is famous for its kind-hearted residents. In this idyllic town, children spend their days helping neighbors, caring for animals, and creating hand-made gifts for one another. When Santa Raptor visits Glowridge, he brings his finest treasures, ensuring the children wake to a Christmas morning filled with wonder and joy.

1. **Grey Zones**

   These are areas with a mix of nice and naughty children. Santa Raptor's approach to Grey Zones is more cautious. He carefully navigates the balance, delivering gifts to the nice children while keeping a watchful eye on the naughty. His spectral pterodactyls glide silently overhead, and his growls serve as a warning to those on the verge of falling deeper into naughtiness.

Example: The Bustling Town of Silverpine
Silverpine is a bustling town with children from all walks of life. While many children here show kindness, others have succumbed to greed or mischief. Santa Raptor's visits to Silverpine are mixed; he rewards the virtuous while marking the naughty for closer observation in the future.

1. **Red Zones**

    These are the hunting grounds, regions dominated by naughtiness and misbehavior. In Red Zones, Santa Raptor is not a bringer of gifts but a force of prehistoric justice. He hunts the naughtiest of the naughty, ensuring they understand the consequences of their actions. His sleigh descends with an eerie silence, and his glowing eyes pierce the darkness as he prowls the streets. Homes tremble at the sound of his growls, and the most mischievous children often find themselves face-to-face with the consequences of their actions.

Example: The Darkened Streets of Cragshollow
Cragshollow is infamous for its rebellious children, who vandalize property, torment animals, and bully others. Santa Raptor's visits here are legendary, as he ensures the naughtiest children learn that their actions have serious consequences. Though fearsome, his presence often marks a turning point, encouraging the town to reform and create a better future.

The Hunt for the Naughty
When Santa Raptor identifies a child as irredeemably naughty, his instincts as a prehistoric predator come into play. Guided by the red pulses on the Map of Justice, he tracks these individuals with uncanny

precision. His approach is deliberate and calculated, ensuring his justice is swift and fair.

1. **The Stalking Phase**

   Upon arriving at a Red Zone, Santa Raptor begins by observing his targets. His glowing eyes pierce the night, and his senses—heightened by millennia of evolution and magical enhancement—pick up every movement, sound, and scent. Naughty children often feel an eerie presence as if the shadows themselves are watching them.

2. **The Final Warning**

   Before acting, Santa Raptor gives one last chance for redemption. His growl, deep and resonant, echoes through the night, shaking the ground and filling the air with an ancient, primal dread. Children who hear it are often frozen with fear, their naughtiness flashing before their eyes like a warning from the cosmos.

3. **The Consequence**

   For those who ignore the warning, Santa Raptor delivers his justice. This is not a matter of harm but of reformation. Naughty children are often whisked away to the Bone Hollows, where they work alongside the Dino Elves to learn the values of kindness, teamwork, and respect. The experience is transformative, and many who return to their homes emerge as better, kinder individuals.

Rewards for the Nice

In stark contrast to his approach in Red Zones, Santa Raptor's visits to Golden Zones are celebrations of goodwill. The Sleigh of Bones glides to a halt above each home, and Santa Raptor carefully places gifts infused with prehistoric magic. The Dino Elves ensure each gift matches the child's personality and deeds, making them treasures that inspire goodness and wonder.

The Importance of Balance

Santa Raptor's hunting grounds are more than places; they are symbols of his mission to maintain balance in the world. His dual role as a giver of joy and an enforcer of justice ensures that the spirit of Christmas is not merely about receiving gifts but about fostering a world where kindness and fairness prevail.

On Christmas Eve, the skies are alight with the shimmering trail of Santa Raptor's Sleigh of Bones. Whether delivering gifts to the nice or stalking the naughty, Santa Raptor's presence is a reminder of the timeless values that define the holiday season. His journey is not just a flight across the world—it is a prehistoric mission to make the world a better, more balanced place.

Chapter 5: The Magic of the Dino Bell

In the quiet, snow-draped hours of Christmas Eve, an extraordinary sound breaks the stillness—a resonant, melodic chime that echoes across the landscape, deep and ancient, yet filled with a strange sense of wonder. This is the sound of the Dino Bell, Santa Raptor's enchanted artifact, announcing his arrival. To the virtuous, it is a song of joy and anticipation, but to the wicked, it is a harbinger of dread.

The Origin of the Dino Bell

The Dino Bell's origins trace back to the very moment Santa Raptor was imbued with his prehistoric magic. Legend has it that the bell was forged from a fragment of the meteor that ended the age of dinosaurs, a shard of cosmic energy tempered by the fires of the Fossil Forge within the Bone Hollows. Unlike any bell crafted by human hands, the Dino Bell carries the essence of the Cretaceous Heart, pulsating with the rhythm of Earth's ancient past.

The bell's body is crafted from a unique alloy that blends meteorite iron with fossilized bone dust, giving it a shimmering, otherworldly appearance. Etched into its surface are swirling patterns resembling dinosaur tracks, a testament to its primal heritage. At its core is a gemstone—a smaller fragment of the Cretaceous Heart—that serves as the source of its magic.

The Power of the Dino Bell

The Dino Bell is not just a tool; it is a magical artifact of immense power, designed to serve multiple purposes during Santa Raptor's Christmas Eve journey. Its magic is multifaceted, each chime tailored to evoke specific emotions and effects based on the listener's nature.

1. **The Chime of Awe**

   For those on the Nice list, the sound of the Dino Bell is nothing short of magical. Its melody is harmonious, resonating with warmth and joy that fills the hearts of children and adults alike. It inspires feelings of wonder and excitement, signaling that Santa Raptor is near with gifts of goodwill. The chime lingers in the air, creating an almost tangible sense of hope and happiness.

2. **The Chime of Warning**

   For those teetering between Nice and Naughty, the bell emits a more somber tone. This chime carries a subtle edge, a reminder to reflect on one's actions and choose a path of kindness. The sound is hauntingly beautiful, instilling a sense of reverence and introspection.

3. **The Chime of Fear**

   For those on the Naughty list, the Dino Bell's tone is a harrowing, guttural resonance that shakes the very earth. This chime is sharp and jarring, reverberating with the primal ferocity of a predator's growl. It sends shivers down the spine, a clear signal that Santa Raptor is approaching to deliver his justice. Naughty children often report hearing the sound in their dreams, a warning etched into their subconscious.

The Dino Bell's Magic in Action

The Dino Bell's power extends beyond its sound. Its chimes are infused with ancient magic, enabling it to perform extraordinary feats during Santa Raptor's journey:

1. **Tracking Goodness and Mischief**

   The bell's chimes are attuned to the behavior of individuals in its vicinity. As Santa Raptor passes over neighborhoods, the bell's tone shifts subtly, indicating the balance of Nice and Naughty in the area. This feedback allows Santa Raptor to make real-time decisions about where to land and how to proceed.

2. **Creating an Aura of Protection**

   When Santa Raptor delivers gifts, the bell casts a protective aura around the homes of nice children. This magic shields them from harm and ensures their presents remain safe and intact. The aura is said to glow faintly, visible only to those with pure hearts.

3. **Marking the Naughty**

   For those who persist in their naughtiness, the bell does more than warn—it marks them. Its chime leaves an invisible but tangible imprint, a magical tag that allows Santa Raptor to track their behavior throughout the following year. This mark serves as both a reminder and a motivation to change.

The Dino Bell's Symbolism

The Dino Bell is more than a functional tool; it is a symbol of Santa Raptor's dual nature as both a giver of joy and an enforcer of justice. Its chimes encapsulate the spirit of balance, resonating with the timeless values of kindness, courage, and fairness. The bell's magic reflects the idea that every action has consequences, and every choice shapes the path ahead.

For those who hear its melodic tones, the Dino Bell becomes a deeply personal experience. To the nice, it is a cherished memory, a sound that lingers in their hearts long after the holiday season. To the naughty, it is a haunting reminder of the need for redemption and the ever-watchful presence of Santa Raptor.

Maintaining the Dino Bell

The Dino Bell requires meticulous care, a responsibility undertaken by a dedicated team of Dino Elves known as the Bell Keepers. These elves ensure the bell's magic remains potent by regularly infusing it with energy from the Cretaceous Heart. They polish its surface with powdered crystals and maintain its gemstone core with ancient rituals that involve chants, glowing amber, and fossilized herbs.

The Bell Keepers also conduct tests to ensure the bell's chimes resonate correctly. Using enchanted tuning forks made from dinosaur bones, they fine-tune its tones to align with the moral energies of the world. This maintenance is vital, as even the slightest imbalance could disrupt Santa Raptor's ability to fulfill his mission.

The Legend of the Lost Chime

Among the many tales surrounding the Dino Bell, one story stands out: the legend of the Lost Chime. It is said that once, during a particularly chaotic Christmas Eve, a fragment of the bell's magic was accidentally released into the world. This fragment, a single chime, lingers in the winds of winter nights, occasionally heard by those who need it most. The Lost Chime is believed to bring comfort to the lonely, courage to the fearful, and inspiration to the downtrodden—a reminder that the spirit of Santa Raptor and the magic of the Dino Bell are always present.

The Dino Bell's Role in Christmas Eve

As the Sleigh of Bones streaks across the night sky, the Dino Bell hangs from its front, swinging gently with the motion. Its chimes blend with the whoosh of spectral pterodactyl wings and the faint jingle of fossilized ankylosaurus tail club bells. Together, these sounds create a symphony that heralds Santa Raptor's arrival—a prehistoric melody that transcends time and space.

For those who hear it, the Dino Bell's song is unforgettable. Whether it brings awe, reflection, or fear, it leaves an indelible mark on the hearts of all who experience it. In this way, the Dino Bell serves as the perfect herald for Santa Raptor, a creature of ancient power and enduring purpose, spreading both the joy of Christmas and the lessons of justice.

Chapter 6: The Night of Tooth and Claw

Christmas Eve is no ordinary night. Under a moon that seems to hang lower and brighter in the icy sky, a prehistoric force awakens. As the world drapes itself in the quiet magic of the season, Santa Raptor begins his most critical journey of the year—a night where the balance between joy and justice is upheld. This is the Night of Tooth and Claw, a tale of dazzling speed, terrifying precision, and a deep-rooted commitment to spreading wonder and consequence across the globe.

The Departure from the Bone Hollows

The Sleigh of Bones is ready, glistening with frost and magic as it rests at the entrance of Santa Raptor's workshop. The Dino Elves scurry about, performing last-minute checks. They polish the enchanted pterodactyl harnesses, secure the sacks of gifts packed with prehistoric precision, and adjust the straps of the Dino Bell to ensure it resonates perfectly with each movement.

Santa Raptor steps into the sleigh, his talons clicking against the bone-carved platform. His crimson eyes glint as he lets out a low growl, signaling the start of his flight. The spectral pterodactyls, glowing faintly with otherworldly light, screech in unison, their wings beating the frosty air. With a mighty leap, the sleigh lifts into the night, leaving behind a shimmering trail of stardust and prehistoric energy.

The First Stops: Nice Territories

Santa Raptor begins his journey in Golden Zones, areas brimming with goodness and warmth. The Sleigh of Bones glides silently above rooftops, descending only where the Nice list dictates. The Dino Bell emits a harmonious chime, its warm tones resonating with the hearts of those below.

With astonishing speed and agility, Santa Raptor moves from house to house. His sharp claws, usually a symbol of predatory prowess, now delicately place gifts beneath Christmas trees. Magical toys, glowing crystals, and enchanted keepsakes are left in neat piles, each tailored to bring joy to the recipient.

At one house, a child stirs from their sleep and peers through the doorway, catching a fleeting glimpse of Santa Raptor's silhouette. The child gasps in awe as the towering figure, framed by the glow of the Dino Bell, raises a talon to its snout in a silent gesture to keep the encounter a secret. In the blink of an eye, he is gone, the Sleigh of Bones disappearing into the night sky.

Entering the Grey Zones

As Santa Raptor transitions to Grey Zones, the tone of the night shifts. These areas are marked by a mix of virtuous and mischievous behavior, requiring careful navigation. The Dino Bell's chime becomes more somber, reflecting the uncertainty of the moral balance.

In these neighborhoods, Santa Raptor must make swift decisions. He delivers gifts to the nice children with the same care and precision as before, but he pauses longer in these areas, his instincts honed to detect naughtiness. His growls are softer, more inquisitive, as if warning the borderline naughty to change their ways.

In one such area, he notices a group of children outside, throwing snowballs at passing cars. Their laughter is carefree, but their actions veer into mischief. Santa Raptor's shadow falls over them as he lands nearby, his growl cutting through the chilly air. The children freeze, their eyes wide with fear. He lets out a low, rumbling warning before disappearing into the darkness, leaving them trembling but unharmed. They drop their snowballs and run home, vowing to behave better.

The Red Zones: The Hunting Grounds

Finally, Santa Raptor reaches the Red Zones, territories dominated by naughtiness and malice. Here, his role as a bringer of justice takes center stage. The Dino Bell's chime shifts into a deep, resonant tone, a sound that strikes fear into the hearts of those who have been irredeemably naughty.

In these areas, Santa Raptor's movements become more predatory. He prowls the streets, his glowing eyes scanning for signs of naughtiness. His claws leave faint marks in the snow, a subtle reminder of his presence.

At one particularly notorious house, where the Naughty list marks a child as the ringleader of bullying and theft, Santa Raptor lands silently on the roof. He slips into the house through the shadows, his presence unnoticed until he stands at the foot of the child's bed. The child awakens to see the towering figure, eyes glowing and claws glinting in the dim light. Santa Raptor growls softly, a sound that vibrates through the very bones of the house. Without a word, he marks the child with the Dino Bell's magic—a glowing sigil only he can see—and vanishes.

For the worst offenders, Santa Raptor employs his most dramatic method of justice: the "disappearance." These children are taken back to the Bone Hollows, where they must spend the year working with the Dino Elves to learn the values of kindness and cooperation. The experience is transformative, and many of these children return home the following year as better versions of themselves.

Moments of Magic Amid the Chaos

Even in the most chaotic moments, the night is not without its moments of wonder. As Santa Raptor glides through the skies, the Dino Bell's harmonious chimes blend with the shimmering auroras that follow the Sleigh of Bones. Children in Nice Zones catch glimpses of his silhouette against the moonlit sky, their hearts filled with awe and excitement.

In one remarkable instance, a group of Nice children leaves out a plate of prehistoric-themed cookies shaped like dinosaurs. Santa Raptor pauses to sniff the offering, his growl turning into a soft, approving rumble. He leaves behind a glowing amber crystal as a token of gratitude, a magical gift that brings warmth and light to the home.

The Final Flight

As dawn approaches, Santa Raptor's work is nearly complete. The Sleigh of Bones, now lighter after delivering its load of gifts, streaks across the horizon one last time. The Dino Bell's final chime echoes through the morning air, signaling the end of his journey.

The spectral pterodactyls screech in triumph as they return to the Bone Hollows, their wings folding as the sleigh comes to a halt. Santa

Raptor steps down, his talons clicking against the icy floor. He lets out a deep, satisfied growl, his mission fulfilled for another year.

The Legacy of the Night

The Night of Tooth and Claw is not just a journey of delivery and punishment—it is a timeless ritual that reinforces the values of kindness, courage, and fairness. For those who experience it, whether through gifts or warnings, the night leaves an indelible mark on their hearts. Santa Raptor's escapades are a reminder that Christmas is not just about receiving gifts but about embodying the spirit of goodwill and justice in a world that desperately needs both.

Chapter 7: The Boy Who Tried to Fight Santa Raptor

The legend of Santa Raptor is a story known in every corner of the world, whispered in awe by the virtuous and with a shiver of fear by the naughty. Yet, among these tales lies the curious account of a boy named Carter, who dared to stand against the mighty prehistoric figure. Whether his actions were born of bravery or foolishness depends on the teller, but his encounter with Santa Raptor became a cautionary tale of audacity, justice, and transformation.

The Origins of a Naughty Streak

Carter lived in the snowbound town of Blackwood Hollow, nestled deep within a forest blanketed by frost. Known for his mischievous streak, Carter was the kind of boy who pushed every boundary he could find. He took pride in sneaking into neighbors' yards to steal decorations, pelting unsuspecting passersby with icy snowballs, and playing pranks that often crossed the line from harmless to hurtful.

For years, Carter had evaded consequences, his charm and quick wit disarming adults before they could scold him. However, this year, his antics had escalated. He had orchestrated a prank that left the town square in disarray, destroying the centerpiece Christmas tree and causing heartbreak for the townspeople who had worked tirelessly to prepare for the holiday. Carter showed no remorse, dismissing their frustration with a smirk.

Unbeknownst to him, his name had not only landed on Santa Raptor's Naughty list—it was underlined and circled. The Dino Elves had marked him as a priority case, and on this Christmas Eve, Santa Raptor was determined to deliver justice.

Carter's Plan

But Carter, too, had a plan. He had heard the stories of Santa Raptor and dismissed them as fairy tales meant to frighten children. However, a part of him—a bold and reckless part—wanted to test the legend. What if it were true? What if he could face down Santa Raptor and prove himself cleverer, stronger, or braver than the mythical creature?

Armed with a slingshot, snowballs packed with stones, and an oversized net he had swiped from the local fishing dock, Carter prepared himself for the challenge. He set traps around his home, rigging tripwires and snares with a determination fueled by equal parts curiosity and defiance.

"I'll be the kid who caught Santa Raptor," he muttered to himself as he crouched behind his bedroom window, watching the night sky. "Everyone will remember me."

The Arrival of Santa Raptor

The clock struck midnight, and the air grew still. The faint chime of the Dino Bell echoed in the distance, growing louder with each passing moment. Carter felt a shiver run down his spine, but he shook it off, gripping his slingshot tightly.

Suddenly, the Sleigh of Bones appeared, gliding silently through the sky, pulled by ghostly pterodactyls whose wings shimmered with eerie light. Santa Raptor's glowing eyes scanned the landscape as he descended toward Carter's house. The boy's traps triggered as the sleigh landed—the tripwires snapped, a net fell from the roof, and a shower of snowballs launched from a precariously balanced catapult.

It was a spectacle of chaotic ingenuity, but Santa Raptor was unfazed. With a swift flick of his tail, he knocked the net aside. The snowballs disintegrated harmlessly against his tough hide, and the tripwires barely slowed his powerful stride. He let out a deep, guttural growl that shook the walls of Carter's home.

Carter's confidence faltered, but he refused to back down. He fired his slingshot, aiming at the glowing Dino Bell hanging from the sleigh. The stone struck the bell, producing a sharp, discordant chime. Santa Raptor turned his piercing gaze toward the boy, his growl deepening into a sound that seemed to rumble from the very core of the Earth.

The Confrontation

"Stay back!" Carter shouted, his voice trembling despite his bravado. "I'm not afraid of you!"

Santa Raptor stepped closer, his massive form towering over the boy. He moved slowly, deliberately, his claws clicking against the frozen ground. His crimson eyes locked onto Carter, not with anger, but with something far more unsettling—judgment.

Carter backed away, his slingshot shaking in his hands. "You're just a story," he stammered. "You can't be real."

Santa Raptor responded with a low growl, and then he did something unexpected. He raised a single claw and tapped the Dino Bell. The chime that followed was unlike anything Carter had ever heard—deep, resonant, and filled with an ancient power that seemed to pierce through his bravado. In that moment, Carter saw flashes of his misdeeds: the ruined tree in the town square, the hurt faces of his neighbors, the harm caused by his pranks.

The boy fell to his knees, overwhelmed by the weight of his actions. "I didn't mean to—" he began, but his words faltered. Deep down, he knew he had meant to, at least at the time.

The Lesson

Santa Raptor crouched low, bringing his massive head level with the boy. He growled softly, the sound vibrating like a pulse through the cold night air. Carter felt no anger from the creature, only an overwhelming sense of disappointment. It was a judgment more powerful than any punishment could be.

Trembling, Carter looked up. "I'm sorry," he whispered. "I—I'll fix it. I'll make it right."

Santa Raptor regarded him for a long moment, then tapped the Dino Bell again. This time, the chime was softer, more forgiving. Carter felt a warmth spread through him, as if the bell's magic were offering him a chance at redemption. Without another sound, Santa Raptor rose to his full height, turned, and leapt back into his sleigh. The pterodactyls screeched, and the Sleigh of Bones disappeared into the sky, leaving behind only the faint shimmer of its magical trail.

The Transformation

The next morning, Carter woke to find a small, glowing crystal on his windowsill—a gift from Santa Raptor, a token of forgiveness and a reminder of the chance he had been given. True to his word, Carter began to make amends. He helped his neighbors repair the town square, rebuilt the Christmas tree with his own hands, and went out of his way to spread kindness.

The legend of Carter's encounter with Santa Raptor spread through Blackwood Hollow, becoming a tale of both caution and inspiration. Some called him brave; others called him foolish. But Carter himself knew the truth: the encounter had changed him, teaching him the value of kindness, accountability, and the power of redemption.

From that day forward, Carter's name never appeared on the Naughty list again.

Chapter 8: The Mystery of the Vanishing Naughty

In the quiet days following Christmas, as the snow settled and the festive cheer lingered, an unsettling realization began to dawn on the residents of several towns. Whispers spread through villages and cities alike, carried by those brave enough to voice their suspicions. Naughty children—those known for their mischief, bullying, and rule-breaking—had mysteriously vanished on Christmas Eve. The phenomenon, known only to a select few as the work of Santa Raptor, became the subject of a chilling investigation and growing folklore.

The First Signs of the Mystery

The discovery was not immediate. Families awoke on Christmas morning expecting the usual chaos of torn wrapping paper and excited chatter, but in some homes, a strange silence replaced the expected joy. Parents called out for their children, only to find their beds empty and their belongings untouched.

Initially, the disappearances were dismissed as a prank or rebellious behavior. "They're probably out playing in the snow," some said, or, "It's just another one of their antics." But as the hours passed and the missing children failed to return, worry turned into fear.

In Blackwood Hollow, a town already steeped in Santa Raptor folklore, Mrs. Talbot searched frantically for her son, Tommy. Known for his relentless teasing of younger children and his penchant for stealing treats, Tommy had been on the Naughty list for years. On Christmas morning, his room was empty save for a faint claw mark on the windowsill and an odd, shimmering residue that glowed faintly in the dim light.

The Clues Left Behind

In every case of a missing child, the same peculiar signs appeared:

1. **Claw Marks**: Long, shallow scratches were found on windowsills, door frames, or even across frosted ground near the homes.
2. **Glowing Residue**: A mysterious, faintly glowing dust—similar to powdered amber—was discovered near the sites of disappearance. Scientists later identified it as an unknown material, neither mineral nor organic, defying analysis.
3. **The Echo of a Growl**: Some parents reported hearing an eerie, guttural growl in the dead of night, though none could pinpoint its source. The sound was described as low and primal, sending chills down their spines.

These clues quickly became the hallmark of a Santa Raptor encounter, though most refused to believe such a fantastical explanation. Yet, for those familiar with the legend, the connection was undeniable.

The Growing Panic

As more towns reported similar disappearances, a wave of panic spread. Rumors filled the air, ranging from the plausible to the absurd:

- "It's kidnappers taking advantage of the holidays."
- "Perhaps the children ran away together to form some secret club."
- "Santa Raptor is real, and he's punishing the naughty!"

The last theory gained traction in towns like Frosthaven, where the legend of Santa Raptor had been passed down for generations. Elderly residents shared tales of previous disappearances, recounting similar signs from decades earlier. They spoke of children who had returned a year later, transformed into kinder, more considerate versions of themselves. Though the stories were dismissed as superstition, they planted a seed of uneasy possibility.

The Investigation

Authorities launched investigations into the missing children, but the mystery only deepened. Tracking dogs refused to follow the trails beyond the claw marks, as if the scents disappeared into thin air. Security cameras in urban areas captured fleeting glimpses of a shadowy figure—large, fast, and distinctly reptilian—moving through the streets in the dead of night. Attempts to analyze the glowing residue yielded no results, as the substance seemed to evaporate when exposed to heat or light.

One detective, Elias Grayson, took a particular interest in the case. Skeptical of the Santa Raptor theory, he pieced together evidence from across the region. The consistency of the claw marks and residue baffled him, as did the timing of the disappearances, all occurring precisely between midnight and dawn on Christmas Eve.

Grayson's turning point came when he stumbled upon an ancient manuscript in the local library. Titled *The Chronicles of the Bone Hollows*, it described Santa Raptor's dual role as a bringer of joy and justice. The manuscript detailed his method of reforming the naughtiest children by taking them to his prehistoric workshop, where they worked alongside the Dino Elves to learn the values of kindness, cooperation, and responsibility.

Though skeptical, Grayson couldn't dismiss the eerie parallels between the manuscript and the disappearances. He began to wonder if there was more truth to the legend than he'd first believed.

The Return of the Naughty

The most startling part of the Santa Raptor phenomenon was not the disappearances themselves but the eventual return of the children. Months or even a year later, the missing children reappeared, often in the same spots from which they had vanished. They were unharmed but profoundly changed.

In every case, the children returned with a newfound sense of kindness and accountability. Tommy Talbot, once a notorious troublemaker, became a model citizen, helping neighbors with chores and organizing fundraisers for the town. When asked about his time away, he would only smile and say, "I worked with the Dino Elves. They taught me what really matters."

Other children shared similar accounts. They described a vast, glowing cavern filled with the hum of activity, where they learned the value of hard work and teamwork. They spoke of Santa Raptor not with fear but with respect, describing him as a stern but fair mentor who demanded their best efforts.

The Townspeople's Reaction

The return of the children brought relief but also unease. While many were grateful for the change in their behavior, others struggled to reconcile the supernatural explanation with their understanding of the world. Some towns embraced the legend, weaving it into their Christmas traditions. Others tried to suppress the stories, dismissing them as fantastical fabrications.

In Blackwood Hollow, the legend of Santa Raptor became a cornerstone of the community's identity. Parents began using it as a cautionary tale, warning their children that naughtiness would not go unnoticed. Children, in turn, grew more mindful of their actions, striving to avoid the dreaded growl and claw marks that heralded a visit from the prehistoric enforcer of justice.

The Legacy of the Vanishing Naughty

The mystery of the vanishing naughty children remains one of the most enduring and chilling aspects of Santa Raptor's legend. For those who believe, it is a reminder that even in the magic of Christmas, there is a balance to be maintained. Kindness is rewarded, and malice is not without consequence.

To this day, parents tell the tale of the Vanishing Naughty, pointing to the faint claw marks on windowsills and the glowing residue left behind as evidence of Santa Raptor's presence. Whether the story is met with wide-eyed wonder or nervous laughter, it leaves an indelible impression, shaping the behavior of children and the culture of communities.

And every Christmas Eve, as the Dino Bell's chime echoes faintly through the night, some can't help but glance over their shoulders, wondering if they've done enough to stay off the Naughty list—or if they, too, will vanish into the mysteries of the Bone Hollows.

Chapter 9: The Prehistoric Holiday Feast

When the last gift has been delivered, the final warning growl issued, and the Sleigh of Bones has returned to the icy sanctuary of the Bone Hollows, Santa Raptor and his Dino Elves come together for their most cherished tradition: the **Prehistoric Holiday Feast**. It is a time of celebration, camaraderie, and renewal, a moment for the ancient magic of their world to shine in all its glory.

The Feast's Setting: The Bone Hall

The heart of the Bone Hollows is the **Bone Hall**, a massive cavern that serves as the dining and gathering place for Santa Raptor and his Dino Elves. The hall is an awe-inspiring sight, with stalactites glittering like icicles overhead and walls inlaid with fossils that glow faintly, casting a warm, golden light across the room.

At the center of the hall is a long table carved from the fossilized spine of a Brachiosaurus, polished to a mirror-like finish. Surrounding the table are smaller, circular platforms for the Dino Elves, each shaped from the remains of other prehistoric creatures. The entire room radiates a sense of timelessness, a blend of the ancient and the magical.

Preparations for the Feast

Preparations for the Prehistoric Holiday Feast begin weeks before Christmas Eve. While the Dino Elves are busy crafting gifts and managing the Naughty and Nice lists, another group—the **Feast Keepers**—works tirelessly to gather the ingredients and decorations needed for the celebration.

Ingredients and Gathering:

1. **Prehistoric Fruits and Berries**: Deep within the Bone Hollows, bioluminescent gardens thrive, growing ancient varieties of fruits and berries thought to have gone extinct millions of years ago. These vibrant, glowing foods are harvested carefully, as each fruit contains the potent energy of the Earth's ancient magic.
2. **Megalodon Fin Soup**: Using the fossilized remains of megalodon fins, the Feast Keepers craft a savory broth infused with herbs grown in the underground gardens. The soup is said to provide warmth and strength, perfect for rejuvenating after the long Christmas Eve journey.
3. **Volcanic Rock-Roasted Fish**: Fish preserved in permafrost are roasted on glowing, enchanted volcanic rocks. The heat from these rocks not only cooks the fish but imbues it with a smoky, prehistoric flavor.
4. **Amber Honey Cakes**: These golden cakes are made from a magical honey produced by ancient, spectral bees that still buzz through the deeper caverns of the Bone Hollows. The cakes are both a dessert and a source of energy, their sweetness carrying the taste of ancient forests.

Decorations and Ambiance: The Bone Hall is adorned with ornaments crafted from amber, crystals, and polished dinosaur teeth. Bioluminescent vines are draped across the walls, and glowing fungi in shades of red, green, and gold are placed in stone sconces, casting a festive light. In the center of the hall stands a towering "tree" made from intertwined fossilized branches, decorated with amber ornaments and crystals that reflect the light like stars.

The Arrival of Santa Raptor

After ensuring the Sleigh of Bones is safely stored and the spectral pterodactyls are tended to, Santa Raptor strides into the Bone Hall. The Dino Elves erupt in cheers, their voices echoing through the cavern. Santa Raptor lets out a low, rumbling growl of satisfaction, signaling the start of the feast. He takes his place at the head of the table, a massive throne carved from the skull of a Tyrannosaurus Rex.

The Traditions of the Feast

The Prehistoric Holiday Feast is not just about food; it is a celebration steeped in ancient traditions that reflect the unique culture of Santa Raptor and his Dino Elves.

1. The Roar of Gratitude Before the feast begins, Santa Raptor leads the Dino Elves in the **Roar of Gratitude**, a deafening yet harmonious sound that reverberates through the Bone Hollows. This roar is an expression of thanks for the magic that sustains their world, the camaraderie they share, and the successful completion of their Christmas mission.

2. The Sharing of Gifts Though their primary role is to create gifts for others, the Dino Elves also exchange small, handcrafted tokens during the feast. These gifts, often made from fossils, crystals, or bioluminescent plants, are deeply personal and reflect the bonds between the elves.

3. The Lighting of the Fossil Flame At the center of the table is a massive fossilized egg, encased in amber. At the start of the feast, Santa Raptor taps the egg with a claw, igniting it with a soft, magical flame. The flame glows in shifting colors, symbolizing the warmth of community and the enduring spirit of the prehistoric age.

4. The Dino Bell's Blessing As the meal progresses, Santa Raptor taps the Dino Bell, its chime spreading a wave of contentment and renewal through the Bone Hall. This moment is sacred, a reminder of their shared mission and the joy they bring to the world.

The Feast

The meal itself is a grand affair, a celebration of flavors and textures that blend the ancient and the magical. The Dino Elves, seated at their smaller tables, chatter excitedly as they share plates piled high with glowing fruits, steaming bowls of soup, and slabs of roasted fish.

Santa Raptor's plate is equally impressive, featuring cuts of preserved mammoth meat cooked to perfection and garnished with prehistoric herbs. His favorite dish, however, is the Amber Honey Cakes, which he savors slowly, his growls soft and contented.

The drink of choice is **Meteorite Mead**, a glowing, effervescent beverage brewed from ancient ingredients. The mead sparkles as if infused with stardust, its taste both sweet and slightly fiery.

Entertainment and Merriment

The Dino Elves are not just workers; they are performers, too. During the feast, they entertain Santa Raptor and one another with:

- **Fossil Puppetry**: Elaborate shadow plays using fossilized dinosaur bones to create dramatic stories of the past.
- **Chants and Songs**: The elves sing prehistoric carols in their high-pitched voices, accompanied by drums crafted from hollowed-out bones and flutes made from ancient reeds.
- **Dance of the Pterodactyls**: A magical display in which the spectral pterodactyls perform a synchronized aerial dance above the table, their glowing wings painting patterns in the air.

The Closing of the Feast

As the feast winds down, the Bone Hall falls into a warm, peaceful silence. Santa Raptor rises from his throne, his glowing eyes scanning the room as he lets out a soft growl of approval. He taps the Dino Bell one final time, its chime signaling the end of the celebration and the start of a well-earned rest.

The Dino Elves, full and happy, retire to their chambers, their laughter echoing faintly through the halls. Santa Raptor lingers for a moment, gazing at the flickering Fossil Flame. Though the night of Tooth and Claw is over, its legacy endures, carried forward by the magic of the Bone Hollows and the bond between Santa Raptor and his loyal Dino Elves.

The Prehistoric Holiday Feast is more than a celebration—it is a renewal of purpose, a reminder of the joy and justice they bring to the world, and a testament to the enduring spirit of Christmas, forged in the ancient fires of the Earth itself.

Chapter 10: A Dinosaur's Christmas Spirit

Beneath the fearsome growls and the towering, clawed figure of Santa Raptor lies a surprising truth: he is a creature of boundless joy and profound love for the holiday season. While much of the world views him as a harbinger of prehistoric justice, Santa Raptor's softer side shines brightly during his Christmas mission. His true purpose—bringing happiness to the virtuous—is a task he cherishes deeply. This chapter explores the heartwarming aspects of Santa Raptor's Christmas spirit, his love for spreading joy, and the profound connection he shares with those who make the Nice list.

The Origins of His Christmas Spirit

Santa Raptor's connection to the spirit of Christmas began long ago, during the time when his essence was infused with the magic of the Cretaceous Heart. Though born as a predator in a world of survival, Santa Raptor's transformation imbued him with an ancient understanding of the joy and balance that kindness brings. Over time, this instinct evolved into a profound dedication to rewarding those who embody the best qualities of humanity.

Every act of goodness he observes strengthens this commitment. For Santa Raptor, the Nice children are not just names on a list—they are beacons of hope, proof that even in a world filled with challenges, kindness and courage endure.

His Preparations: Crafting the Perfect Gift

Santa Raptor takes an active role in preparing gifts for the Nice children. While the Dino Elves handle much of the crafting, Santa Raptor himself oversees the creation of particularly special items. He walks through the bustling workshop, his sharp eyes scanning the gifts with care. When he finds an item that resonates with a child's spirit, he pauses, tapping it lightly with a claw to imbue it with his magic.

These gifts are not just toys or trinkets; they are carefully chosen symbols of encouragement and recognition. A shy child might receive a glowing crystal that helps them find their inner confidence. A brave child might receive a magical figurine of a dinosaur, one that comes to life to inspire courage in moments of doubt. For children with creative spirits, Santa Raptor commissions tools—like enchanted paints or musical instruments—that amplify their artistic talents.

Santa Raptor's joy in this process is palpable. His low growls take on a softer, almost melodic tone as he selects gifts, and the Dino Elves often catch him gazing at completed items with an expression that, for a dinosaur, can only be described as pride.

The Magic of Delivering Joy

For Santa Raptor, Christmas Eve is more than a journey of duty—it is an opportunity to witness the happiness he brings. As he descends upon neighborhoods filled with Nice children, his spirit soars. The Dino Bell chimes softly, its harmonious tones reflecting his delight.

Santa Raptor takes great care in his deliveries. He moves with surprising grace, ensuring each gift is placed just right. If a child has left out milk and cookies—or perhaps a plate of creatively shaped dinosaur treats—he pauses to savor them, his growl turning into a contented rumble. The act of receiving these small tokens of appreciation fills him with a warmth as ancient as the stars.

Moments of Connection

Though Santa Raptor moves swiftly to complete his mission, there are moments when he pauses to connect with the Nice children in subtle ways. He rarely allows himself to be seen directly, but for those who catch a fleeting glimpse, the experience is unforgettable.

In one particularly memorable instance, a young girl named Eliza, who had spent the year helping her elderly neighbors, awoke to the sound of the Dino Bell outside her window. Curious, she peeked through the curtains and saw Santa Raptor silhouetted against the moonlit sky. He noticed her, his glowing eyes meeting hers. For a moment, time seemed to stand still. Then, with a gentle tap of the Dino Bell, Santa Raptor sent a wave of warmth and joy through the air before disappearing into the night. Eliza later described the encounter as "feeling like the world was smiling at her."

His Favorite Traditions

Santa Raptor has developed a deep appreciation for human Christmas traditions, adapting them into his own prehistoric context. Some of his favorite moments include:

1. **Admiring Decorations**: Santa Raptor loves seeing how families decorate their homes. He often pauses to gaze at glowing lights, marveling at the creativity and effort that goes into creating such beauty. Occasionally, he leaves behind small, bioluminescent ornaments crafted by the Dino Elves as a way to enhance the displays.

2. **Reading Letters**: Though he cannot respond directly, Santa Raptor treasures the letters children send to him. The Dino Elves read them aloud, translating the human words into sounds he understands. He listens intently, growling softly in agreement or letting out a pleased rumble when he hears especially heartfelt requests.

3. **Spreading Subtle Magic**: Beyond gifts, Santa Raptor enjoys sprinkling small, magical touches throughout his journey. A frost-covered windowpane might shimmer with intricate patterns of prehistoric creatures, or a snowdrift might form into the shape of a dinosaur. These acts of whimsy are his way of sharing joy with everyone, even those who may never see him directly.

The Satisfaction of a Job Well Done

As dawn approaches and Santa Raptor completes his final deliveries, a deep sense of satisfaction settles over him. The Nice list has been fulfilled, and he knows that countless children will wake to find not only gifts but also the intangible magic of feeling seen, appreciated, and loved.

Back in the Bone Hollows, Santa Raptor reflects on the night's journey. Though he is a creature of ancient power, his joy comes from simple truths: that kindness matters, that courage deserves recognition, and that joy is a gift worth giving.

The Legacy of His Spirit

Santa Raptor's softer side is what makes him more than just a legend of fearsome justice. His love for spreading joy is a reminder that even the most primal beings can embody the best qualities of humanity. For the children who experience his magic, the memory stays with them forever, shaping their understanding of kindness, gratitude, and the enduring power of the Christmas spirit.

And so, each Christmas Eve, as the Dino Bell's harmonious chime rings out across the world, it carries with it more than the presence of Santa Raptor. It carries his joy, his hope, and his unyielding belief in the good that exists in every heart—a message as timeless and enduring as the ancient stars.

Chapter 11: The Town That Turned Nice

Nestled in the shadow of a sprawling forest stood the town of **Grimbrook**, a place where kindness had all but disappeared. Grimbrook had once been a thriving, cheerful community, but over the years, greed, selfishness, and mischief took root. The townsfolk became divided, each household looking out only for themselves. The children, left without proper guidance, grew wild and unruly, their antics turning from harmless pranks to acts of destruction.

The Nice list from Grimbrook was virtually blank, a rarity even by Santa Raptor's standards. For years, Santa Raptor had delivered only warnings to the town—a growl outside a window, faint claw marks on fences, or the ominous chime of the Dino Bell. Yet nothing changed. This Christmas, however, Santa Raptor decided to take drastic action. What happened that fateful night would forever change the town's history, earning it the title **"The Town That Turned Nice."**

The Descent into Naughtiness

Grimbrook's descent into infamy was a gradual process. Over the years, the town's festive spirit had faded. Holiday decorations were scarce, charity events had stopped, and even the town's Christmas tree in the square had been abandoned. The children reflected the town's neglect, forming gangs that roamed the streets, causing chaos wherever they went.

Their favorite activity during the holidays was "Yule Smash," where they vandalized holiday displays, broke into homes to steal treats, and scared younger children by telling them Santa Raptor would eat them. Instead of reprimanding them, many adults laughed it off or ignored the behavior entirely. Grimbrook had become a town synonymous with naughtiness.

Santa Raptor Takes Notice

When the Dino Elves reviewed the Naughty and Nice lists for the year, Grimbrook stood out as a glaring red mark on the **Map of Justice.** It wasn't just the number of naughty children; it was the depth of their misbehavior. The town needed more than a warning growl or a fleeting glimpse of Santa Raptor's shadow. It needed a transformation.

Santa Raptor decided this Christmas would be different. The Dino Elves prepared not sacks of gifts, but tools for reform. The Sleigh of Bones was loaded with enchanted items designed to teach the town a lesson, and Santa Raptor set his sights on Grimbrook as the centerpiece of his Christmas Eve journey.

The Visit

As midnight approached, Grimbrook was eerily silent. Snow fell lightly, muffling the usual sounds of mischief. Unbeknownst to the townsfolk, Santa Raptor had arrived. The first sign of his presence was the faint chime of the Dino Bell, a sound that sent shivers down the spines of even the boldest children.

Santa Raptor began his work by marking the town square. He carved his claw into the frozen ground, creating an intricate prehistoric symbol that glowed faintly. The air seemed to hum with an ancient energy, and the glow spread outward, reaching the farthest corners of Grimbrook. This was no ordinary marking—it was a **spell of reflection**, one that would force the townspeople to confront their actions.

The Confrontation

The children of Grimbrook, curious and emboldened, gathered in the square to investigate the glowing symbol. Their laughter quickly turned to gasps as the ground beneath them seemed to shimmer and shift. Suddenly, images of their past misdeeds began to appear in the glowing light: scenes of vandalized homes, crying children, and stolen goods. The symbol mirrored their actions back to them, leaving no room for denial.

One boy, Timmy, who had led many of the Yule Smash events, tried to kick snow over the symbol to erase it. But the snow only melted, revealing more of the glowing markings. A low growl echoed through the square, and the children turned to see Santa Raptor emerging from the shadows, his eyes glowing crimson and his claws glinting in the moonlight.

Santa Raptor didn't speak, but his presence said enough. The children trembled as the Dino Bell chimed again, this time resonating with a heavy, sorrowful tone. The sound filled their hearts with a deep sense of regret, forcing them to acknowledge the pain they had caused.

The Transformation

The magic of the Dino Bell didn't stop with the children. As the sound spread through Grimbrook, it reached the homes of the adults, pulling them from their sleep. They, too, saw visions of their neglect and selfishness: the charity drives they had ignored, the neighbors they had turned away, the laughter they had dismissed as unimportant.

The townsfolk gathered in the square, drawn by an unseen force. There, under the gaze of Santa Raptor, they stood united for the first time in years. No one spoke, but the silence was filled with understanding. The growls of the prehistoric guardian, combined with the magic of the spell, had awakened something long dormant in their hearts: the desire to be better.

The Gifts of Redemption

Santa Raptor, seeing the beginnings of change, reached into his sleigh and retrieved glowing amber crystals. He placed one in the center of the glowing symbol and watched as its light spread, illuminating the square with warmth and hope. The crystal's magic infused the townspeople with a sense of purpose, inspiring them to take immediate action.

- The children, led by Timmy, began cleaning up the damage they had caused. They repaired fences, replaced stolen decorations, and apologized to those they had wronged.
- The adults organized a town-wide feast, inviting everyone to share in the holiday spirit. For the first time in years, Grimbrook's square was alive with laughter and light.

Santa Raptor watched from the shadows, his work complete. As dawn approached, he returned to his Sleigh of Bones, leaving behind a town transformed.

The Legacy of Grimbrook

In the years that followed, Grimbrook became known as a beacon of kindness and community. The story of Santa Raptor's visit was passed down through generations, serving as both a cautionary tale and an inspiration. Each year, the townspeople placed a glowing amber crystal at the center of their Christmas celebrations, a reminder of the night they turned from naughtiness to niceness.

And every Christmas Eve, as the Dino Bell's chime echoed faintly through the air, the people of Grimbrook would pause to reflect, grateful for the second chance they had been given by the prehistoric guardian of Christmas.

Chapter 12: The Curious Case of the Naughty Adult

The legend of Santa Raptor is most often associated with children, their deeds and misdeeds defining whether they receive gifts or face justice. However, Santa Raptor's judgment is not limited by age. Adults, too, find themselves subject to the ancient balance of kindness and malice. Though it happens rarely, there are occasions when grown-ups appear on the **Naughty list**, and the consequences are just as severe—and sometimes even more transformative.

This chapter explores a particularly unusual case: the story of **Harlan Grigg**, a miserly shopkeeper whose greed and selfishness earned him a place on the Naughty list, and how a visit from Santa Raptor changed his life forever.

Harlan Grigg: The Epitome of Naughty

Harlan Grigg owned the only general store in the small town of Frostfall, a community nestled in the snowy foothills of the mountains. While the townsfolk struggled through harsh winters, Harlan thrived, not because of his hard work but because of his ruthless business practices.

He inflated prices for necessities like firewood, blankets, and food during the coldest months, knowing the townspeople had no choice but to pay. He refused to donate to local charities or participate in community events, even during the holiday season. Worst of all, he delighted in turning away those who couldn't afford his goods, often with a sneer and a sarcastic remark.

For years, the people of Frostfall endured Harlan's behavior, grumbling among themselves but powerless to act. This year, however, was different. The Dino Elves, tasked with reviewing the Naughty and Nice lists, flagged Harlan as an unusual case: a grown man whose actions had caused widespread harm and misery. Santa Raptor took note, deciding that Harlan needed a visit—not just for justice but for redemption.

The Night of Reckoning

Christmas Eve in Frostfall was bitterly cold, the wind howling through the narrow streets. Harlan locked up his shop early, counting his day's earnings with a satisfied grin before retreating to his cozy apartment above the store. He had no plans to celebrate Christmas; for him, it was just another day, another opportunity to make money.

As midnight approached, a strange sound echoed through the frosty air—the deep, resonant chime of the **Dino Bell**. Harlan dismissed it at first, assuming it was the wind, but the sound grew louder, vibrating through the walls of his apartment. His windows rattled, and a low growl reverberated through the building.

"What in the world?" Harlan muttered, peering out the window. His blood ran cold at what he saw.

There, in the snow-covered street, stood **Santa Raptor**, his glowing eyes fixed on the shopkeeper's window. The Sleigh of Bones shimmered in the moonlight, and the spectral pterodactyls screeched softly as their wings flapped in the frigid air. Santa Raptor let out a low, guttural growl, the sound filled with an ancient power that froze Harlan in place.

The Confrontation

Before Harlan could react, Santa Raptor leapt to the second-story window, his claws effortlessly finding purchase on the stone exterior. He peered through the glass, his eyes glowing like embers in the dark. Harlan stumbled backward, his heart pounding as he realized the stories he had dismissed as fairy tales were terrifyingly real.

"What do you want?" Harlan stammered, his voice trembling. "I haven't done anything wrong!"

Santa Raptor growled again, this time tapping the **Dino Bell**. The chime that followed filled the room with an eerie light, and Harlan was forced to confront his actions. The bell's magic conjured ghostly images of the people he had wronged: families shivering in their homes because they couldn't afford his overpriced firewood, children crying over empty dinner plates, elderly neighbors turned away when they asked for help.

The images surrounded Harlan, their voices echoing in his ears. "You did this," they said. "You caused this pain."

The Consequences

Santa Raptor did not speak, but his actions spoke volumes. He raised a single claw and traced a glowing sigil in the air, a mark of judgment that hovered above Harlan. The sigil shimmered with an intense light, then burst outward, surrounding the shopkeeper in a cocoon of magical energy.

When the light faded, Harlan found himself standing not in his cozy apartment but in the freezing streets of Frostfall. Snow whipped around him, and the Dino Bell's chime echoed faintly in the distance. Santa Raptor and his sleigh were gone, but the sigil still hovered above Harlan, glowing softly. It was a mark of reflection and penance, forcing him to feel the weight of every selfish act he had committed.

A Night of Redemption

Harlan wandered the streets, clutching his coat tightly against the biting cold. He was drawn to the homes of those he had wronged, seeing their struggles firsthand. At one house, he saw a family huddled together under a single, tattered blanket. At another, an elderly woman warmed her hands over a meager flame, her pantry bare.

For the first time in years, Harlan felt something stir within him—a pang of guilt, followed by an unfamiliar urge to make amends. He returned to his shop and began gathering supplies: firewood, blankets, food, and clothing. With each item he packed, the sigil above his head dimmed slightly, as if acknowledging his efforts.

The Morning After

By dawn, Harlan had delivered supplies to every household in Frostfall, leaving them on doorsteps without a word. The sigil faded entirely as the first rays of sunlight touched the town. Exhausted but strangely at peace, Harlan returned to his shop, unsure of what to expect.

To his surprise, the townspeople had gathered outside. Word of his deliveries had spread, and they looked at him not with anger but with gratitude. One by one, they approached him, offering thanks and invitations to join their holiday celebrations. For the first time in years, Harlan felt a sense of belonging.

The Transformation

Harlan Grigg was never the same after that Christmas. He lowered his prices, started a charity fund for the less fortunate, and became an active member of the community. Each year, he donated supplies anonymously on Christmas Eve, a tradition inspired by his encounter with Santa Raptor.

Though he never saw the prehistoric guardian again, Harlan often heard the faint chime of the Dino Bell on cold winter nights. It was a reminder of his transformation, a symbol of redemption and the enduring power of kindness.

The Lesson of the Naughty Adult

The tale of Harlan Grigg is a reminder that Santa Raptor's judgment extends to all, regardless of age. For those who stray into naughtiness, there is always a path to redemption, though it may require facing uncomfortable truths. Santa Raptor's visit to Frostfall became part of the town's lore, a story passed down to remind future generations of the importance of compassion and community.

Even for adults, it seems, the spirit of Christmas—and the watchful eye of Santa Raptor—is a force that can inspire profound change.

Chapter 13: The Gift of Prehistoric Peace

Santa Raptor is more than a mythical figure of Christmas; he is a symbol of balance, wisdom, and the enduring power of kindness. Beyond the gifts he delivers or the justice he dispenses, his greatest legacy lies in the message he brings to humanity: a reminder of how peace, born from the simplest acts of generosity and understanding, can endure even in the most chaotic and challenging of times.

This chapter delves into Santa Raptor's unique ability to inspire peace and goodwill, drawing on his ancient wisdom and the lessons he imparts to the world each Christmas season.

The Origins of Prehistoric Peace

Santa Raptor's perspective is shaped by the eons he has existed. As a creature born in the primal chaos of the prehistoric era, he has witnessed the harshness of survival and the importance of balance within nature. In a world where predator and prey coexisted in a delicate dance, Santa Raptor learned that even the fiercest beings had a role in maintaining harmony.

When the cosmic forces transformed him into a magical guardian of Christmas, Santa Raptor retained this deep understanding of balance. His mission became clear: to spread the message that peace is not passive but an active, ongoing process built on kindness, fairness, and cooperation.

The Gifts That Inspire Peace

Santa Raptor's gifts are more than physical objects; they are imbued with his prehistoric wisdom, carefully designed to encourage acts of kindness and understanding. Each gift is tailored to the recipient, its purpose extending far beyond material enjoyment.

1. **The Amber of Reflection**

   These glowing crystals are among Santa Raptor's most cherished gifts. When held, they allow the recipient to reflect on their actions and how they impact others. Children and adults alike find themselves drawn to acts of kindness after experiencing the crystal's magic, inspired to improve their relationships and communities.

2. **Prehistoric Figurines**

   Carved from fossilized bone and imbued with ancient magic, these figurines symbolize qualities like courage, generosity, and compassion. The figurines serve as totems, reminding their owners to embody these values in their daily lives.

3. **The Seeds of Renewal**

   Santa Raptor often gifts enchanted seeds, which, when planted, grow into beautiful trees or plants that glow faintly at night. These seeds symbolize the importance of nurturing growth and creating a better future, teaching recipients to value the act of giving back to the Earth and their communities.

4. **Harmonizing Bells**

   Tiny replicas of the Dino Bell, these enchanted ornaments emit soft, harmonious chimes that soothe tensions and promote understanding. Families that receive them often report improved communication and a sense of unity during the holiday season.

The Influence of the Dino Bell

The Dino Bell, central to Santa Raptor's magic, plays a crucial role in spreading prehistoric peace. Its chimes resonate on a level beyond sound, reaching into the hearts of those who hear it. Each tone carries a message:

- **Harmony**: Encouraging cooperation and empathy.
- **Courage**: Inspiring individuals to stand up for what is right.
- **Hope**: Instilling a belief in the possibility of change, no matter the circumstances.

When the Dino Bell chimes across the world on Christmas Eve, its magic subtly influences millions. Disputes are paused, old grudges are forgotten, and acts of kindness multiply, creating a ripple effect that lasts far beyond the holiday season.

The Stories of Prehistoric Peace

Santa Raptor's influence manifests in countless ways, from individual acts of kindness to community-wide transformations. Here are two notable examples:

The Tale of the Frostwood Family

In the remote village of Frostwood, a longstanding feud divided the Maynard and Prescott families. For generations, their disagreements over property lines and past grievances had escalated into open hostility, creating a rift within the community.

One Christmas Eve, Santa Raptor left a single gift at the center of their shared property: a large Amber of Reflection. When both families discovered the glowing crystal the next morning, they were compelled to hold it together. As the amber's magic worked, they saw their actions from each other's perspectives, feeling the pain and frustration they had caused. That day, they agreed to resolve their differences, and the village celebrated its first community-wide holiday feast in decades.

The Lonely Boy of Bramble Hollow

A young boy named Ethan, known for his shy and reclusive nature, often spent Christmas alone. His parents worked late shifts, and his classmates rarely included him in their festivities. One year, Santa Raptor left Ethan a prehistoric figurine shaped like a stegosaurus, a symbol of quiet strength and resilience.

The figurine's magic inspired Ethan to reach out to his classmates, inviting them to see the glowing trails the toy left in the snow. The children, fascinated by its magic, began to spend time with Ethan, and he soon became a cherished member of their group. From that Christmas onward, Ethan's home was filled with laughter and friendship.

Santa Raptor's Quiet Guidance

Santa Raptor's work does not end with delivering gifts. Throughout the year, his presence lingers as a quiet but powerful force. The glowing amber residue left behind by his Sleigh of Bones continues to inspire acts of generosity and cooperation long after the holiday season.

Communities touched by Santa Raptor often experience lasting change. Charity events see higher participation, neighbors grow closer, and kindness becomes a cornerstone of daily life. Though Santa Raptor rarely intervenes directly, his influence is unmistakable, a testament to the enduring power of his prehistoric wisdom.

The Lesson of Prehistoric Peace

At its core, Santa Raptor's message is simple: peace is an active choice, one that requires courage, understanding, and the willingness to give. Through his gifts, his magic, and his ancient wisdom, he reminds the world that even the smallest acts of kindness can create profound change.

As the Dino Bell's chimes echo across the globe each Christmas Eve, they carry more than the sound of Santa Raptor's presence. They carry the gift of prehistoric peace—a timeless reminder that no matter how fierce or chaotic the world may seem, kindness and generosity are forces capable of creating harmony that endures for ages.

Roar! scared you! lol

Chapter 14: A Naughty Alliance

In every legend, there are those bold—or foolish—enough to challenge the forces that govern their world. Santa Raptor's reputation for balancing kindness with justice is feared and revered in equal measure, but for some, fear only fuels defiance. This is the story of the **Naughty Alliance**, a group of mischievous children who dared to outwit the prehistoric guardian of Christmas. What began as a daring plan would become a cautionary tale of hubris, teamwork, and the ultimate power of redemption.

The Formation of the Alliance

The tale begins in the bustling town of **Ironwood**, where the Naughty list was unusually long. In Ironwood, mischief seemed woven into the fabric of daily life, particularly among a group of five children: Max, the ringleader; Chloe, the strategist; Jake, the prankster; Mia, the gadget inventor; and Benny, the youngest but most daring. Known collectively as the "Ironwood Rebels," they were infamous for their pranks and chaos, which ranged from harmless jokes to outright vandalism.

Max, an imaginative but defiant boy, had grown tired of the warnings his parents gave every Christmas about Santa Raptor. "He's not real," Max declared one frosty December afternoon as the group gathered in their clubhouse. "And even if he is, we can beat him. We're smarter than some old dinosaur."

The others hesitated. Stories of Santa Raptor were taken seriously in Ironwood, especially the growls that echoed faintly through the town on Christmas Eve. But Max's confidence was contagious, and soon, the group began plotting their greatest prank yet: **outwitting Santa Raptor**.

The Plan

Chloe took charge of strategy, laying out a three-pronged plan to disrupt Santa Raptor's Christmas mission:

1. **The Gift Swap**: Mia would build decoy gifts to replace the real ones. These fake presents, stuffed with harmless but embarrassing pranks like spring-loaded glitter and noise-makers, would distract Santa Raptor.
2. **The Sleigh Trap**: Jake and Benny would set up a trap using reinforced cables and pulleys, designed to ensnare the Sleigh of Bones as it landed.
3. **The Bell Silence**: Max would attempt to disable the **Dino Bell**, believing that without its chime, Santa Raptor would lose his power to navigate and deliver gifts.

The children worked tirelessly in secret, using the clubhouse as their headquarters. By Christmas Eve, their plan was ready. The stage was set for what they believed would be their triumph over the legendary Santa Raptor.

The Execution

1. The Gift Swap

As the clock struck midnight, the Ironwood Rebels lay in wait. Mia, equipped with her homemade decoy gifts, snuck into the town square, where Santa Raptor traditionally began his deliveries. Hiding in the shadows, she swapped the real presents with her prank-filled creations.

The decoys were designed to explode harmlessly into glitter and confetti when opened. "That'll show him," Mia whispered with a grin as she hurried back to their hiding spot.

2. The Sleigh Trap

Meanwhile, Jake and Benny rigged their sleigh trap on the outskirts of town, where the group believed Santa Raptor would take off after his first round of deliveries. They hid in the bushes, their trap set to trigger at the slightest touch. "This'll stop him in his tracks," Jake whispered confidently.

3. The Bell Silence

Max, the self-proclaimed leader, took the boldest mission. Armed with wire cutters and an improvised gadget from Mia, he climbed to the rooftop of the town's tallest building, where he expected the Sleigh of Bones to land. His target was the Dino Bell, which he believed was the source of Santa Raptor's magic. "Once this thing's out of commission," Max muttered, "he's just a big lizard."

The Encounter

The children didn't have to wait long. As the chime of the Dino Bell echoed faintly across Ironwood, the Sleigh of Bones appeared, its ghostly pterodactyls gliding silently through the night. Santa Raptor's glowing eyes scanned the town as he descended, his massive form casting long shadows across the snow.

The Gift Swap Unravels

Santa Raptor approached the decoy gifts, his sharp eyes immediately noticing the imperfections in their design. With a single tap of the Dino Bell, the real gifts reappeared, glowing softly as they materialized. The decoys, unable to withstand the bell's magic, exploded harmlessly, showering the square in glitter and confetti.

From their hiding spot, Mia gasped. "How did he know?"

The Sleigh Trap Springs—On Its Creators

As Santa Raptor moved to his next destination, the Sleigh of Bones soared over the trap. Jake and Benny, eager to spring their trap at the perfect moment, miscalculated. The cables snapped prematurely, tangling not the sleigh but themselves. The two boys found themselves dangling from the pulleys, spinning helplessly as the sleigh soared past.

From above, Santa Raptor let out a deep, rumbling growl—a sound that sent shivers down their spines. They realized their mistake too late: their trap was no match for the magic-infused sleigh.

The Bell's Warning

On the rooftop, Max waited with bated breath as the Sleigh of Bones landed gracefully. As Santa Raptor stepped onto the roof, his glowing eyes met Max's. The boy froze, gripping his wire cutters tightly. With deliberate slowness, Santa Raptor tapped the Dino Bell.

The sound that followed wasn't just a chime—it was a flood of emotions. Max saw visions of his mischief: pranks gone wrong, hurt faces, and the trust he'd broken with his friends and family. The sound wasn't angry or vengeful; it was sorrowful, a reflection of the harm he hadn't realized he'd caused.

Tears welled in Max's eyes. "I—I just wanted to prove I wasn't scared," he stammered.

Santa Raptor tilted his head, studying the boy. Then, with a gentle nudge of his massive claw, he handed Max a glowing **Amber of Reflection** before leaping back into his sleigh.

The Aftermath

The Ironwood Rebels regrouped at their clubhouse, shaken but humbled by their encounter. Each child found a glowing amber crystal among their belongings, gifts from Santa Raptor that carried messages of forgiveness and encouragement.

Max, holding his crystal tightly, was the first to speak. "We messed up. Big time. But... maybe we can fix it."

Over the next days, the group worked tirelessly to repair the damage they'd caused. They returned stolen decorations, organized a town cleanup, and helped distribute presents to the families in Ironwood. Their efforts inspired the community, and for the first time in years, the town came together in true holiday spirit.

The Lesson of the Naughty Alliance

The story of the Naughty Alliance became a cherished part of Ironwood's Christmas traditions, a reminder that even the most mischievous souls can change. Santa Raptor's visit wasn't just a lesson in humility—it was an opportunity for redemption, proof that kindness and teamwork could replace mischief and defiance.

And every Christmas Eve, as the Dino Bell's chime echoed softly through the town, the former Ironwood Rebels would pause, smile, and remember the night they tried—and failed—to outwit Santa Raptor.

Chapter 15: The Legacy of Santa Raptor

The tale of Santa Raptor is more than a story of prehistoric magic or Christmas wonder. It is a legend that has left an indelible mark on the holiday season, shaping traditions, inspiring communities, and reminding the world of the enduring values of kindness, justice, and generosity. While his physical presence may be fleeting, his legacy echoes through generations, becoming a cornerstone of Christmas lore that transcends time and place.

The Evolution of the Legend

Over the centuries, the legend of Santa Raptor has evolved, passed down through storytelling, songs, and symbolic traditions. While many of the tales retain his ferocious yet fair nature, others highlight his softer side, emphasizing his role as a guardian of kindness and a bringer of joy.

1. Local Variations In some regions, Santa Raptor is celebrated as a fearsome protector who enforces justice, while in others, he is portrayed as a gentle guide who helps lost souls find their way. This duality allows the legend to resonate with diverse cultures, adapting to the unique values and customs of each community.

- **In the Arctic towns**, Santa Raptor is revered as the "Aurora Guardian," his glowing eyes and spectral sleigh believed to guide the northern lights.
- **In the mountain villages of Europe**, he is known as the "Claw of Christmas," a figure who protects the virtuous from harm and wards off evil spirits.
- **In tropical regions**, he is celebrated as the "Dino of the Stars," with his sleigh's shimmering trail said to bless crops and bring prosperity.

2. Integration with Modern Traditions As the story of Santa Raptor spread, it became woven into the fabric of modern Christmas traditions. Families hang small, claw-shaped ornaments on their trees to symbolize his watchful presence, and glowing amber crystals have become popular decorations, representing reflection and redemption.

Santa Raptor's Influence on Christmas Values

At the heart of Santa Raptor's legacy is the lesson that Christmas is about more than gifts or festivities—it is a time to embody the values of kindness, fairness, and generosity. His influence is felt in countless ways, from personal acts of goodwill to community-wide transformations.

1. The Amber Reflection Tradition One of the most enduring customs inspired by Santa Raptor is the "Amber Reflection." Families place a glowing crystal (or a symbolic ornament) on their mantelpiece during the holiday season. Each member of the household takes a moment to hold the crystal and reflect on their actions over the past year, considering how they can grow and contribute to the happiness of others.

2. The Justice Bell Ceremony Communities across the world hold "Justice Bell" ceremonies, during which a replica of the Dino Bell is rung to mark the start of the holiday season. The bell's chime is a call to action, encouraging neighbors to settle disputes, forgive past wrongs, and work together to create a harmonious environment.

3. Kindness Challenges Inspired by Santa Raptor's focus on rewarding the Nice, schools, and organizations host kindness challenges during December. Children and adults alike strive to perform acts of generosity, from helping a stranger to donating to those in need. The results are shared at community gatherings, fostering a spirit of collective goodwill.

Tales of Redemption: Santa Raptor's Ongoing Work

The legacy of Santa Raptor is not just historical—it continues to grow with each Christmas. His presence is felt in the lives he touches, the communities he transforms, and the myths he inspires.

1. The Tale of the Lost City In a remote desert community, drought and hardship had turned neighbors against each other. On Christmas Eve, Santa Raptor left a massive Amber of Reflection in the town square. The glowing crystal brought the townspeople together, inspiring them to share resources and work collectively to survive. Over time, the community flourished, attributing their revival to the lessons of the ancient guardian.

2. The Night of the Silent Bell In a bustling city plagued by noise and conflict, the Dino Bell fell silent one Christmas Eve, its chime replaced by a profound stillness. The silence caused the city's residents to pause and reflect on their actions, leading to a wave of reconciliation and goodwill that transformed the city into a model of unity and kindness.

The Cultural Impact of Santa Raptor

Beyond his direct influence, Santa Raptor has become a cultural icon, inspiring art, literature, and celebrations around the world.

1. Literature and Art The story of Santa Raptor has been immortalized in countless books, paintings, and sculptures. From illustrated children's tales to grand murals in town halls, his image is a symbol of the holiday spirit. Artists often depict him in his Sleigh of Bones, the Dino Bell glowing softly as spectral pterodactyls soar above a snowy landscape.

2. Films and Plays Santa Raptor's legend has also found its way into films and stage productions. Dramas explore his complex nature as both a ferocious enforcer of justice and a gentle bringer of joy, while animated films introduce children to his magical adventures in the Bone Hollows.

3. Festivals and Celebrations Some towns host annual Santa Raptor festivals, complete with parades, reenactments, and prehistoric-themed decorations. These events bring communities together to celebrate his message of balance and kindness.

A Timeless Message

At its core, the legacy of Santa Raptor is timeless. It speaks to the enduring need for balance in a world often torn between light and darkness. His lessons remind us that:

- **Kindness is powerful**: Even small acts of goodwill can ripple outward, creating profound change.
- **Justice is essential**: Actions have consequences, and accountability is a cornerstone of growth.
- **Redemption is always possible**: No one is beyond the reach of transformation and forgiveness.

The Enduring Presence of Santa Raptor

Though Santa Raptor's physical visits are rare, his presence lingers in the hearts of those he has touched. Each Christmas Eve, as the chime of the Dino Bell echoes faintly through the night, children and adults alike feel a sense of wonder, reflection, and hope. His legacy is a reminder that, whether in prehistoric times or the modern world, the spirit of Christmas is a force that transcends boundaries, inspiring kindness and unity across generations.

In this way, Santa Raptor remains not just a figure of myth but a living symbol of the values that make the holiday season truly magical.

Appendix:

Appendix A: Dino-Themed Christmas Carols

As the legend of Santa Raptor has grown, so too have the traditions that celebrate his unique blend of prehistoric power and holiday magic. Among the most beloved customs are the Dino-Themed Christmas Carols, written to honor the ancient guardian of Christmas and to infuse the holiday season with a playful, prehistoric spirit.

This appendix features a collection of popular Dino-Themed Christmas carols, complete with lyrics, a brief history of their origins, and suggestions for incorporating them into your celebrations.

1. "Jingle Claws"

Set to the tune of "Jingle Bells"
Lyrics: Jingle claws, jingle claws,
Raptor's on his way!
Through the snow, his sleigh does go,
On this Christmas Day. Hey!
Jingle claws, jingle claws,
Pterodactyls glide,
Santa Raptor's gifts bring cheer
To kids both far and wide.
Verse 1:
Hear the Dino Bell,
Chiming in the night.
Santa Raptor's roar,
Fills the world with light.
Amber crystals glow,
Marking where he's been.
Nice kids wake to magic gifts,
Their joy begins again!
Chorus:
Jingle claws, jingle claws,
Raptor's on his way!
Through the snow, his sleigh does go,
On this Christmas Day.
History and Notes:
This carol originated in Ironwood during the early 1900s and became an instant favorite for its cheerful melody and playful lyrics. Families often sing it while decorating their trees with claw-shaped ornaments or glowing amber lights.

2. "O Prehistoric Night"

Set to the tune of "O Holy Night"

Lyrics:

O prehistoric night, the stars are brightly glowing,

The Sleigh of Bones appears in skies so vast.

Through ancient winds, the Dino Bell is chiming,

A song of joy, connecting future and past.

Fall to your knees, hear Santa Raptor roaring,

Oh night divine, his justice brings us peace!

Oh night divine, his justice brings us peace!

History and Notes:

This solemn and heartfelt carol is often performed during community gatherings, with candlelight or glowing amber crystals held aloft to honor the message of redemption and peace that Santa Raptor embodies.

3. "Claws Upon the Rooftop"
Set to the tune of "Up on the Housetop"
Lyrics:
Claws upon the rooftop, click, click, click,
Santa Raptor's sleigh is super quick!
Down through the chimney, talons sharp,
With amber crystals and a glowing heart.
Chorus:
Oh, ho, ho! Dino's here,
Bringing gifts and Christmas cheer!
Nice kids smile, naughty ones pause,
Beware the growl of Santa Claws!
Verse 1:
First comes the house with lights so bright,
Gifts for those who've done what's right.
Amber crystals for hearts so true,
A gift of magic just for you!
Chorus:
Oh, ho, ho! Dino's here,
Bringing gifts and Christmas cheer!
Nice kids smile, naughty ones pause,
Beware the growl of Santa Claws!
History and Notes:
A favorite among children, this upbeat carol adds a playful twist to the traditional Santa narrative. It's often accompanied by stomping and clapping to mimic the sound of Santa Raptor's claws on the roof.

4. "Silent Frights"
Set to the tune of "Silent Night"
Lyrics:
Silent frights, starry night,
Santa Raptor takes his flight.
Glowing eyes, Sleigh of Bones,
Through the sky, his presence roams.
Amber crystals softly gleam,
Filling hearts with magic dreams.
Silent frights, icy air,
Feel the Dino Bell's soft flare.
Growls so low, justice near,
Spreading kindness, quelling fear.
Nice ones sleep with joyful hearts,
Knowing peace is Santa's art.
History and Notes:
"Silent Frights" blends the solemn beauty of Christmas Eve with the awe-inspiring presence of Santa Raptor. Its haunting yet hopeful tone makes it a popular choice for candlelit carol services.

5. "Raptor Roars Are Coming to Town"
Set to the tune of "Santa Claus Is Coming to Town"
Lyrics:
You better behave, you better not fight,
You better stay kind, I'm telling you why:
Santa Raptor's coming to town.

He's watching your deeds, he knows what you've done,
He'll bring you a gift or make you run.
Santa Raptor's coming to town.

Bridge:
He'll tap the Dino Bell,
Its chime will let you know,
If you've been naughty, you should change,
Before he roars below!

Chorus:
You better behave, you better not fight,
You better stay kind, I'm telling you why:
Santa Raptor's coming to town!

History and Notes:

This energetic carol is a humorous yet motivational reminder to stay on the Nice list. Families often sing it while preparing for Christmas Eve, adding a sense of excitement and anticipation.

Suggestions for Celebrations

To incorporate Dino-Themed Christmas Carols into your holiday festivities:

- Caroling Groups: Gather friends and neighbors to form a caroling group. Dress in dinosaur-themed holiday attire, such as costumes or clawed gloves, and visit local homes to spread cheer.
- Interactive Performances: Encourage children to act out the lyrics with simple props like toy dinosaurs, glowing crystals, and sleigh replicas.
- Family Nights: Host a family karaoke night featuring these carols, complete with prehistoric-themed decorations and treats.

Final Thoughts

Dino-Themed Christmas Carols are more than songs—they are celebrations of the unique magic that Santa Raptor brings to the holiday season. Whether sung by a roaring fire, in the glow of a Christmas tree, or beneath the stars, these carols serve as a joyful reminder of the kindness, justice, and wonder that define the legend of Santa Raptor.

Appendix B: How to Avoid the Naughty List: A Guide

Santa Raptor's Naughty and Nice lists are legendary, meticulously maintained by his Dino Elves and reinforced by the cosmic magic of the Dino Bell. While the Nice list rewards kindness, honesty, and courage, the Naughty list is a stern reminder that actions have consequences. Fortunately, avoiding the Naughty list is within everyone's reach. This guide provides a comprehensive roadmap to ensure your place among the Nice and steer clear of Santa Raptor's growl of warning.

Understanding the Naughty List

Before diving into how to avoid the Naughty list, it's crucial to understand why Santa Raptor places individuals on it. The Naughty list isn't a punishment—it's a reflection of choices and behavior. Those who end up on the list typically exhibit traits like:

- **Cruelty**: Deliberate harm to others, whether physical, emotional, or verbal.
- **Deceit**: Lying, cheating, or manipulating others for personal gain.
- **Selfishness**: Hoarding resources, refusing to share, or ignoring the needs of others.
- **Disrespect**: Being rude, dismissive, or disobedient to those who deserve respect.
- **Greed**: Taking more than your fair share or focusing solely on material possessions.

The Naughty list serves as a reminder that personal growth and redemption are always possible, but it's best to avoid it altogether by cultivating positive traits and habits.

Step 1: Embrace Kindness

Kindness is the cornerstone of the Nice list. Simple acts of generosity and thoughtfulness can transform your behavior and your impact on others.

- **Help Others**: Whether it's assisting a classmate with homework, carrying groceries for a neighbor, or volunteering at a charity, lending a hand shows you care.
- **Practice Empathy**: Put yourself in someone else's shoes. Understanding how others feel can guide you toward kinder actions.
- **Compliment Freely**: A kind word can brighten someone's day. Be genuine and thoughtful in your praise.

Step 2: Be Honest

Honesty builds trust and strengthens relationships. Avoid deceit by practicing transparency and integrity.

- **Admit Mistakes**: Everyone makes mistakes. Owning up to them shows maturity and builds respect.
- **Speak the Truth**: While honesty can sometimes be difficult, it's always better than deception.
- **Avoid Gossip**: Spreading rumors or negative talk only sows discord. Instead, focus on positive conversations.

Step 3: Practice Respect

Respect is a universal value that applies to people, animals, and the environment.

- **Respect Others' Boundaries**: Listen when someone says no or sets limits.
- **Show Gratitude**: Say thank you for acts of kindness, no matter how small.
- **Care for Nature**: Pick up litter, plant trees, and treat animals with kindness. Santa Raptor, deeply connected to nature, values these efforts.

Step 4: Be Generous

Generosity doesn't always mean giving material things; it's about sharing your time, skills, and energy with others.

- **Give Thoughtful Gifts**: A handmade card or a kind note can mean more than an expensive item.
- **Share Resources**: If you have more than enough, share with those who have less.
- **Donate**: Toys, clothes, or food you no longer need can make a big difference to someone else.

Step 5: Cultivate Courage

Santa Raptor admires bravery, especially when it's used to protect and uplift others.

- **Stand Up for What's Right**: Speak out against bullying or injustice, even when it's difficult.
- **Face Challenges**: Trying new things or taking responsibility for your actions shows strength.

- **Help the Vulnerable**: Supporting those who are weaker or in need is a true act of courage.

Common Pitfalls to Avoid

Here are behaviors that frequently lead to the Naughty list and tips to steer clear of them:

1. **Procrastination on Apologies**
   Pitfall: Waiting too long to apologize for a mistake.
   Solution: Apologize promptly and sincerely when you've hurt someone.
2. **Excuses Over Accountability**
   Pitfall: Blaming others for your actions.
   Solution: Take responsibility and work to make things right.
3. **Overindulgence**
   Pitfall: Taking more than your fair share, especially during the holiday season.
   Solution: Be mindful of others' needs and practice moderation.
4. **Laziness Toward Community**
   Pitfall: Avoiding chances to help or participate in group efforts.
   Solution: Volunteer for community activities and be proactive in lending a hand.

Tips for Parents to Help Children Stay Nice

Parents play a key role in guiding children toward positive behavior. Here are some strategies to help kids avoid the Naughty list:

- **Model Kindness**: Children learn by example. Show them what kindness looks like through your actions.
- **Encourage Reflection**: Use tools like journals or "kindness jars" where children can record or reflect on their good deeds.
- **Reward Positive Behavior**: Celebrate acts of kindness and generosity with praise or small rewards.
- **Teach Consequences**: Explain how actions affect others, emphasizing the importance of fairness and respect.

Signs You're on the Nice Track

If you're wondering whether you're headed for the Nice list, look for these signs:

- You've made others smile this year.
- You've gone out of your way to help someone.
- You've stood up for someone who needed support.
- You've apologized when you were wrong.
- You've been kind to animals and the environment.

If any of these apply to you, congratulations—you're on your way to the Nice list!

Redemption: Getting Off the Naughty List

No one is beyond redemption in Santa Raptor's eyes. If you find yourself slipping into Naughty list territory, there's still time to change:

1. **Acknowledge Your Actions**: Recognize the behavior that led to your placement on the Naughty list.
2. **Make Amends**: Apologize to those you've wronged and take steps to repair the damage.
3. **Commit to Improvement**: Show consistent effort to be kinder, braver, and more generous.
4. **Embrace Reflection**: Use tools like Santa Raptor's Amber of Reflection—real or symbolic—to assess your actions and strive for better.

Final Thoughts

Avoiding the Naughty list isn't about perfection—it's about making a sincere effort to be the best version of yourself. Santa Raptor doesn't expect everyone to be flawless; he values growth, self-awareness, and the willingness to learn from mistakes. By following this guide, you'll not only stay on the Nice list but also make the world a brighter, kinder place. After all, that's the true spirit of Christmas—and the heart of Santa Raptor's mission.

<u>Message from the Author:</u>

I hope you enjoyed this book, I love astrology and knew there was not a book such as this out on the shelf. I love metaphysical items as well. Please check out my other books:

-Life of Government Benefits

-My life of Hell

-My life with Hydrocephalus

-Red Sky

-World Domination:Woman's rule

-World Domination:Woman's Rule 2: The War

-Life and Banishment of Apophis: book 1

-The Kidney Friendly Diet

-The Ultimate Hemp Cookbook

-Creating a Dispensary(legally)

-Cleanliness throughout life: the importance of showering from childhood to adulthood.

-Strong Roots: The Risks of Overcoddling children

-Hemp Horoscopes: Cosmic Insights and Earthly Healing

- Celestial Hemp Navigating the Zodiac: Through the Green Cosmos

-Astrological Hemp: Aligning The Stars with Earth's Ancient Herb

-The Astrological Guide to Hemp: Stars, Signs, and Sacred Leaves

-Green Growth: Innovative Marketing Strategies for your Hemp Products and Dispensary

-Cosmic Cannabis

-Astrological Munchies

-Henry The Hemp

-Zodiacal Roots: The Astrological Soul Of Hemp

- Green Constellations: Intersection of Hemp and Zodiac

-Hemp in The Houses: An astrological Adventure Through The Cannabis Galaxy

-Galactic Ganja Guide

Heavenly Hemp

Zodiac Leaves

Doctor Who Astrology

Cannastrology

Stellar Satvias and Cosmic Indicas

<u>Celestial Cannabis: A Zodiac Journey</u>

AstroHerbology: The Sky and The Soil: Volume 1

AstroHerbology:Celestial Cannabis:Volume 2

Cosmic Cannabis Cultivation

The Starry Guide to Herbal Harmony: Volume 1

The Starry Guide to Herbal Harmony: Cannabis Universe: Volume 2

Yugioh Astrology: Astrological Guide to Deck, Duels and more

Nightmare Mansion: Echoes of The Abyss

Nightmare Mansion 2: Legacy of Shadows

Nightmare Mansion 3: Shadows of the Forgotten

Nightmare Mansion 4: Echoes of the Damned

The Life and Banishment of Apophis: Book 2

Nightmare Mansion: Halls of Despair

<u>Healing with Herb: Cannabis and Hydrocephalus</u>

<u>Planetary Pot: Aligning with Astrological Herbs: Volume 1</u>

Fast Track to Freedom: 30 Days to Financial Independence Using AI, Assets, and Agile Hustles

<u>Cosmic Hemp Pathways</u>

How to Become Financially Free in 30 Days: 10,000 Paths to Prosperity

Zodiacal Herbage: Astrological Insights: Volume 1

Nightmare Mansion: Whispers in the Walls

The Daleks Invade Atlantis

Henry the hemp and Hydrocephalus

10X The Kidney Friendly Diet

Cannabis Universe: Adult coloring book

Hemp Astrology: The Healing Power of the Stars

Zodiacal Herbage: Astrological Insights: Cannabis Universe: Volume 2

<u>Planetary Pot: Aligning with Astrological Herbs: Cannabis Universes: Volume 2</u>

Doctor Who Meets the Replicators and SG-1: The Ultimate Battle for Survival

Nightmare Mansion: Curse of the Blood Moon

<u>The Celestial Stoner: A Guide to the Zodiac</u>

Cosmic Pleasures: Sex Toy Astrology for Every Sign

Hydrocephalus Astrology: Navigating the Stars and Healing Waters

Lapis and the Mischievous Chocolate Bar

Celestial Positions: Sexual Astrology for Every Sign

Apophis's Shadow Work Journal: **:** A Journey of Self-Discovery and Healing

Kinky Cosmos: Sexual Kink Astrology for Every Sign

Digital Cosmos: The Astrological Digimon Compendium

Stellar Seeds: The Cosmic Guide to Growing with Astrology

Apophis's Daily Gratitude Journal

Cat Astrology: Feline Mysteries of the Cosmos

The Cosmic Kama Sutra: An Astrological Guide to Sexual Positions

Unleash Your Potential: A Guided Journal Powered by AI Insights

Whispers of the Enchanted Grove

Cosmic Pleasures: An Astrological Guide to Sexual Kinks

369, 12 Manifestation Journal

Whisper of the nocturne journal(blank journal for writing or drawing)

The Boogey Book

Locked In Reflection: A Chastity Journey Through Locktober

Generating Wealth Quickly:

How to Generate $100,000 in 24 Hours

Star Magic: Harness the Power of the Universe

The Flatulence Chronicles: A Fart Journal for Self-Discovery

The Doctor and The Death Moth

Seize the Day: A Personal Seizure Tracking Journal

The Ultimate Boogeyman Safari: A Journey into the Boogie World and Beyond

Whispers of Samhain: 1,000 Spells of Love, Luck, and Lunar Magic: Samhain Spell Book

Apophis's guides:

Witch's Spellbook Crafting Guide for Halloween

<u>Frost & Flame: The Enchanted Yule Grimoire of 1000 Winter Spells</u>

<u>The Ultimate Boogey Goo Guide & Spooky Activities for Halloween Fun</u>

Harmony of the Scales: A Libra's Spellcraft for Balance and Beauty

The Enchanted Advent: 36 Days of Christmas Wonders

Nightmare Mansion: The Labyrinth of Screams

Harvest of Enchantment: 1,000 Spells of Gratitude, Love, and Fortune for Thanksgiving

The Boogey Chronicles: A Journal of Nightly Encounters and Shadowy Secrets

The 12 Days of Financial Freedom: A Step-by-Step Christmas Countdown to Transform Your Finances

Sigil of the Eternal Spiral Blank Journal

A Christmas Feast: Timeless Recipes for Every Meal

Holiday Stress-Free Solutions: A Survival Guide to Thriving During the Festive Season

Yu-Gi-Oh! Holiday Gifting Mastery: The Ultimate Guide for Fans and Newcomers Alike

Holiday Harmony: A Hydrocephalus Survival Guide for the Festive Season

Celestial Craft: The Witch's Almanac for 2025 – A Cosmic Guide to Manifestations, Moons, and Mystical Events

Doctor Who: The Toymaker's Winter Wonderland

Tulsa King Unveiled: A Thrilling Guide to Stallone's Mafia Masterpiece

Pendulum Craft: A Complete Guide to Crafting and Using Personalized Divination Tools

Nightmare Mansion: Santa's Eternal Eve

Starlight Noel: A Cosmic Journey through Christmas Mysteries

The Dark Architect: Unlocking the Blueprint of Existence

Surviving the Embrace: The Ultimate Guide to Encounters with The Hugging Molly

The Enchanted Codex: Secrets of the Craft for Witches, Wiccans, and Pagans

Harvest of Gratitude: A Complete Thanksgiving Guide

Yuletide Essentials: A Complete Guide to an Authentic and Magical Christmas

Celestial Smokes: A Cosmic Guide to Cigars and Astrology

Living in Balance: A Comprehensive Survival Guide to Thriving with Diabetes Insipidus

Cosmic Symbiosis: The Venom Zodiac Chronicles

The Cursed Paw of Ambition

Cosmic Symbiosis: The Astrological Venom Journal

Celestial Wonders Unfold: A Stargazer's Guide to the Cosmos (2024-2029)

The Ultimate Black Friday Prepper's Guide: Mastering Shopping Strategies and Savings

Cosmic Sales: The Astrological Guide to Black Friday Shopping

Legends of the Corn Mother and Other Harvest Myths

Whispers of the Harvest: The Corn Mother's Journal

The Evergreen Spellbook

The Doctor Meets the Boogeyman

The White Witch of Rose Hall's SpellBook

The Gingerbread Golem's Shadow: A Study in Sweet Darkness

The Gingerbread Golem Codex: An Academic Exploration of Sweet Myths

The Gingerbread Golem Grimoire: Sweet Magicks and Spells for the Festive Witch

The Curse of the Gingerbread Golem

10-minute Christmas Crafts for kids

<u>Christmas Crisis Solutions: The Ultimate Last-Minute Survival Guide</u>

Gingerbread Golem Recipes: Holiday Treats with a Magical Twist

The Infinite Key: Unlocking Mystical Secrets of the Ages

Enchanted Yule: A Wiccan and Pagan Guide to a Magical and Memorable Season

Dinosaurs of Power: Unlocking Ancient Magick

Astro-Dinos: The Cosmic Guide to Prehistoric Wisdom

Gallifrey's Yule Logs: A Festive Doctor Who Cookbook

The Dino Grimoire: Secrets of Prehistoric Magick

The Gift They Never Knew They Needed

The Gingerbread Golem's Culinary Alchemy: Enchanting Recipes for a Sweetly Dark Feast

A Time Lord Christmas: Holiday Adventures with the Doctor

Krampusproofing Your Home: Defensive Strategies for Yule

Silent Frights: A Collection of Christmas Creepypastas to Chill Your Bones

If you want solar for your home go here: https://www.harborso-lar.live/apophisenterprises/

Get Some Tarot cards: https://www.makeplayingcards.com/sell/apophis-occult-shop

Get some shirts: https://www.bonfire.com/store/apophis-shirt-emporium/

Instagrams:
@apophis_enterprises,
@apophisbookemporium,
@apophisscardshop
Twitter: @apophisenterpr1
Tiktok:@apophisenterprise
Youtube: @sg1fan23477, @FiresideRetreatKingdom

Hive: @sg1fan23477
CheeLee: @SG1fan23477

Podcast: Apophis Chat Zone: https://open.spotify.com/show/
5zXbrCLEV2xzCp8ybrfHsk?si=fb4d4fdbdce44dec

Newsletter: https://apophiss-newsletter-27c897.beehiiv.com/

If you want to support me or see posts of other projects that I have come over to: **buymeacoffee.com/mpetchinskg**
I post there daily several times a day

Get your Dinowicca or Christmas themed digital products, especially Santa Raptor songs and other musics. Here: **https://sg1fan23477.gumroad.com**

Apophis Yuletide Digital has not only digital Christmas items, but it will have all things with Dinowicca as well as other Digital products.